SNOWY MOUNTAIN NIGHTS

LINDSAY EVANS

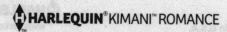

HARLEQUIN® KIMANI™ ROMANCE

Recycling programs
for this product may
not exist in your area.

ISBN-13: 978-0-373-86395-2

Snowy Mountain Nights

Copyright © 2015 by Lindsay Evans

Printed

IN®

com

Lindsay Evans was born in Jamaica and currently lives and writes in Atlanta, Georgia, where she's constantly on the hunt for inspiration, club in hand. She loves good food and romance and would happily travel to the ends of the earth for both. Find out more at lindsayevanswrites.com.

Books by Lindsay Evans

Harlequin Kimani Romance

Pleasure Under the Sun
Sultry Pleasure
Snowy Mountain Nights

Visit the Author Profile page at Harlequin.com for more titles.

To my readers, old and new.
Thank you for sharing your time with me.

Acknowledgments

This new journey of mine wouldn't be possible without Sheree L. Greer, Angela Gabriel and Dorothy Lindsay. As my beta reader, Sheree has read more romance novels than she'd ever even thought possible and Angela has suffered with me through many plotting sessions over dinner and ice cream. Dorothy Lindsay has simply *always* been there.

Kimberly Kaye Terry, as ever, thank you.

Chapter 1

"I hope you know that thirty-six-year-old men *can* die from overwork."

Garrison Richards's secretary, Anthea, walked into his office and put an envelope on his desk. He looked up from scribbling on the yellow legal pad, surprised at the darkness that had fallen outside his windows.

He didn't dignify her comment with an answer. But she apparently didn't need him to say anything.

"Your train ticket and other essentials are right here." She tapped the envelope with a manicured finger. "The weekend at the resort is already paid for. Your train leaves at eight in the morning."

He put down his pen and glanced at his watch, frowning. It was much later than he thought. Nearly ten o'clock. New York, a bright and glittering jewel, flashed in its beautiful finery from his twentieth-story view.

"Are you kicking me out of my own office on a Thursday night?" he asked.

"Yes, I am. With the help of your mother."

Garrison assumed that his mother had paid for the resort and train tickets, while Anthea made sure his schedule was clear. With *help* like this, who needed a wife?

Anthea stood at his desk with the warm overhead light spilling over her still features, looking more motherly than his actual mother, in her practical gray pantsuit, the spectacles sitting on her gently lined face. She clasped her hands at her waist and watched him with endless patience.

"You have the cabin at the resort for the weekend," she said. "I already had your snowboarding equipment delivered." Anthea lifted a finger to forestall his complaints about missing work. "Since you've been trying to meet with Mrs. Taylor-Rodriguez about the latest draft of the agreement, I also arranged a meeting with her on Sunday afternoon before your train home in the evening."

Garrison considered being firm with his secretary. Putting on the more serious than usual face that had his associates and junior attorneys scurrying to do his bidding. It rarely worked on Anthea, but she would at least know he was serious.

That was one of the reasons he hired her. She was efficient and effective, yes. But he enjoyed immensely that she reflected his inner calm, the calm he wanted to reflect in his office. In nine years, he hadn't once regretted his decision. Even when she insisted on mothering him when no one else was around. Now wasn't the time, though. As usual, he had a lot of work to do.

"All the other work can wait." She pressed the button on the remote that controlled the windows, darkening them so he could no longer see outside to the brilliant nighttime Manhattan skyline. "You've been distracted lately. Your work hasn't started to suffer yet, but it might if you don't take a break. You haven't had a proper vacation in over a year."

Garrison's lips tightened at her observation. Part of her effectiveness lay in that she knew how to reach him. His work was precise and thorough, very efficient, which was one of the reasons he was the top divorce attorney in the state. The idea that he could slip up and compromise his usual standards of excellence gave him pause.

"That's not very fair." He felt like a twelve-year-old boy debating the merits of a punishment.

"Life is not fair, as you're always fond of reminding me." Anthea withdrew to the door. She had left the office earlier at her usual time of five-thirty, but apparently came back to ambush him.

"Go, Garrison." Her faint smile chided him. "These broken marriages can wait until Monday morning."

And so the next morning found him doing what she directed, getting on a train heading north to the Adirondack Mountains. With his overnight bag over one shoulder and a briefcase in hand, he looked like the only person in the first-class car with work in mind. His fellow passengers sat back with drinks already in front of them: mimosas, Bloody Marys and some with just plain coffee.

He passed three women getting themselves settled into a quartet of seats. They were beautiful, he noticed automatically, well-made-up and expensively dressed. The kind of women he'd seen at New York society and industry parties he'd been invited to over the years. He idly wondered if they skied or were simply heading north to bask by winter fireplaces while carefully trained servants tended to their every need. When he passed them, his idle wonderings disappeared.

Garrison tucked away his bag and claimed his seats, two sets facing each other that Anthea had arranged just for him, knowing he didn't like to be crowded. Soon the train began to move, and he sat back to make the most of the ride.

Up ahead of him, he noticed that a fourth woman had joined the group of three he'd passed earlier. This woman was sitting with her back to him and speaking animatedly with her hands. She wore her shoulder-length hair in natural curls that brushed the back of her neck. When she stood to put something in the overhead luggage rack, Garrison noticed that she was tall, maybe even six feet, a height he'd always found…compelling. He admired her voluptuous shape, the way she filled out the long green sweater and the jeans she wore beneath it. His eyes returned to her again and again.

Very occasionally, he thought he heard her low voice above the soothing rumble of the train moving over the tracks. There was something about the woman's voice that pricked an awareness of familiarity in him. But she never turned around.

He wondered if it would be too ridiculous of him to walk past the four women then turn back around just so he could get a glimpse of the mystery siren. He dismissed the idea as quickly as it had come. He wasn't the type to get worked up over a woman, especially one he'd only seen from behind and hadn't even talked to.

When the attendant arrived, he ordered a black coffee and opened one of the files he'd brought with him. Just to have something to work on during the train ride, of course.

"Reyna, I need you to cut his damn name off my body!"

Marceline made a sound of frustration and looked at the inside of her wrist, where she had tattooed her soon-to-be ex-husband's name nearly three years before. Her normally beautiful and serene face was tight from stress. The long hair, twisted at the top of her head and fastened with silver chopsticks, only emphasized the unhealthy gauntness of her features.

Sitting opposite Marceline, Reyna shook her head. "Sorry. I only put them on. I don't take them off." She smoothed her fingers over her friend's wrist then squeezed it with a reassurance she was far from feeling. Marceline's eyes were dark with a pain Reyna hoped never to experience.

Beyond the long windows of the train, the landscape was awash in white—snowcapped mountains, pine trees heavy with late-winter white and gracefully twirling flurries drifting from the sky. Despite the turbulence in her friend, Reyna tried to hold on to the sense of peace the snow gave her.

The train, taking them on their annual single women's trip into the Adirondacks for Valentine's Day, rattled soothingly over the tracks, a sound Reyna had always found meditative. But Marceline, still in the middle of divorce proceedings from the man she thought was the one true love of her life, looked uneasy. As if she'd rather be hidden away in her big Long Island house than heading to a ski vacation with three of her closest friends.

"You can see my skin guy in Manhattan," their friend Bridget said as she came back from the restroom, catching the tail end of their conversation. She had ears like a cat. With her short, coiled hair and big amber eyes, she even looked like one. "He's a dermatologist. I'm sure he can take care of that for you." Bridget wrinkled her freckled nose.

"And how would you know that?" Louisa, who had gone to the restroom with Bridget, walked up behind her. She raised an eyebrow, half in inquiry, half in challenge. Her straightened, shoulder-length hair swung down to hide her face for a moment, then she shoved it back, revealing features that had stopped more than one man in his tracks.

Bridget made a vague gesture to her face. "I had skin issues when I was younger. You all remember that, I'm sure."

"Oh, yes. We remember." Louisa smirked.

The four women had known each other since they were preteens at the same exclusive New York private school. They shared over fifteen years of friendship that had been through just about everything under the sun. Reyna, on scholarship that she and her blue-collar Brooklyn parents had worked hard for. Marceline, newly orphaned and recently arrived from Haiti. Bridget, a trust-fund baby looking for the next exciting thing. And Louisa, already cynical and frighteningly brilliant, intrigued at the idea of friendship with girls so different from her.

With the arrival of the two women, Reyna excused herself to make her own way to the bathroom. The train rocked under her as she walked and lightly touched the seats of the other passengers without stumbling into them. The early-morning train from Penn Station to Saratoga Springs was full—after all it was the Friday before Valentine's Day weekend—but it wasn't overwhelming. The last few seats before the bathroom were even empty.

She loved trains. It was because of her that the four of them took the train up to the resort every year instead of flying. But it was because of Bridget's expensive tastes that they traveled in the first-class car with its wider aisles, Wi-Fi and attendants who regularly came through the car offering everything from coffee to newspapers.

As Reyna neared the bathroom, she noticed a man standing in the aisle. With his back turned to her, he leaned his shoulder against the wall of the moving train, looking as comfortable as if he were in his living room. Or office.

Despite his casual clothes—the gray sweater across his broad shoulders, jeans that lovingly skimmed his body—everything about him shouted business. He held a cell phone to his ear and spoke into it in a low, intent voice that stroked a delicate place deep inside Reyna. An unexpected flutter of attraction took wing in her belly. The man's dark jeans draped over a backside that would be envied in any fitness magazine. Or a woman's bedroom. She bit her lip at the thought.

"I find it extremely difficult to care what he *doesn't* want to do. He had those children with the woman he's leaving behind, and so he has to help support them." His tone rumbled with casual power.

Reyna came up behind him. "Pardon me," she said. "Are you waiting for the bathroom?"

The man turned, and Reyna nearly lost her breath. His intent dark eyes swept her from head to foot in a single, scorching glance that was at odds with his cool demeanor. His face was not handsome; instead it was distractingly sexy with its full mouth, sharp cheekbones and dimpled chin. She knew him.

Garrison Richards.

Memories she'd long ago put behind her came rushing back. Garrison's impassive face as he sat next to her ex-husband at the conference room in his downtown law office. Ian watching her with the eyes of a stranger as if they hadn't spent the past eight years of their lives as man and wife. Reyna's horror when she'd realized just what it was that she had signed in those divorce papers.

She flushed, mortified that she had just been lusting after *Garrison Richards*. That afternoon when they met five years ago, there had been nothing sexy about him. Only an off-putting sternness and judgment that left her cold.

In the rocking car of the train, Garrison's gaze raked over her. She felt it from the tips of her snow boots to her shoulder-length curls that she'd sworn had been presentable when she'd left her apartment. She fought the urge to rearrange her hair. Instead, she touched the necklace at her throat, sliding the silver star along the chain. A habit she had when she was nervous or uncertain.

He tipped the phone away from his ear and replied to her earlier question.

"The bathroom is empty. You can go ahead." Directed toward her, his voice was even more compelling, a deep and seductive rumble.

He moved back to allow her to walk past him and into the bathroom. The door rattled shut, and the lock clicked. Reyna took a deep breath as she stared at herself in the mirror. She looked calm and in control, but her cheeks were blazing with heat—a combination of embarrassment and the unwelcome attraction she felt for the man who had represented her husband in their divorce.

She quickly used the bathroom and pushed Garrison from her mind. Afterward, Reyna splashed some water on her face and took her time toweling her skin dry. She desperately hoped he wasn't near the bathroom anymore.

But when she walked out, he was still nearby and still on the phone. But he had stepped away from the door to give her some room. He stared intently at her again and said something to the person on the other end of the phone before speaking to her.

"You look familiar," he said. "Do I know you?"

Reyna ruthlessly shoved the attraction aside and gave him her most scornful look. "No, you don't."

With that, she walked past him and made her way back to her friends.

Chapter 2

Garrison stared after the woman while his secretary's words on the other end of the line fell away from him in a garble of sound. She was the same one he had been watching from before. Now that he'd seen her face, she was breathtaking: an Amazon with a hauntingly beautiful face and body. He drew a quiet breath, hypnotized by the sway of her hips under the green sweater and jeans as she walked away. Halfway down the train, she sat down with her three friends, never once glancing back at him.

"Garrison, are you still there?"

It took him a few seconds to realize Anthea was trying to get his attention. He mentally shook himself.

"My apologies, Anthea. I'm right here."

He finished going over the particulars of the Reichman divorce, yet another rich client who didn't want to financially support his offspring, then went back to his seat. He could hear the muted strains of the woman and her friends' conversation from where he sat. And he wasn't the only man glancing in their direction. Annoyed with himself for his uncharacteristic fascination, Garrison opened a folder for a case still in arbitration, but couldn't concentrate on a single word.

The woman's eyes haunted him. They were black and intense, her gaze as regal and unflinching as a queen's. He drew a swift breath of surprise as he abruptly recalled who she was and how he knew her.

Reyna. Reyna Barbieri.

He'd handled her divorce from her actor husband nearly five years ago. From the look on her face, she had undoubtedly known who he was on sight. And she hadn't been happy to see him.

Garrison remembered the first time he saw her. Ian Barbieri, a client of his whose ship had come in the form of a syndicated crime drama, was a few years into the TV show when he filed for divorce. Every fall, his face was on billboards all over New York City, advertising the new season of his show.

With his star burning bright through the network TV sky, Barbieri had breezed into Garrison's office wanting a quick and surgical separation from his wife of nearly nine years. Garrison hadn't been surprised. Although Ian Barbieri was a relatively small fish in the show business pond in New York, the rumor had been going around for months—with pictures included—that he was cheating on his high school sweetheart. He left her to keep the home fires burning while he had sex with nearly every wannabe starlet and groupie in the city. What had surprised Garrison was that Barbieri's wife hadn't hired a lawyer of her own. Neither had she objected to any of the terms of the divorce that her ex proposed.

Garrison drafted the documents with the stipulations Barbieri wanted and arranged a meeting with the wife thinking that, since the divorce was uncontested, it would be an easy and quick process. Barbieri wanted to keep just about everything he'd made and acquired since the marriage, leaving his wife with nothing but her wedding ring. She hadn't protested.

Then Reyna Barbieri walked into the conference room. Given Barbieri's movie-star looks, Garrison had been prepared for a similar creature, perfectly coiffed and artificial, the New York version of Hollywood. But Reyna had that wholesome loveliness that came from a life lived apart from show business. The air in his lungs stuttered at her natural, long-legged beauty. And the misery in her face.

Her shoulders were slumped. The floral summer dress and light sweater were too insubstantial for the fall weather and too big for her body. The wounded and defenseless look of her made him want to protect her. Garrison wanted to pull her into his arms and shelter her from everything that he knew was to come.

His heart thumped viciously at the unusual wave of feeling. He sat in his chair staring at Reyna as if she were the only person in the room. Garrison was surprised that everyone else hadn't stared at *him* for his blatantly fatuous and unprofessional behavior.

He realized then that despite her husband's flagrant cheating, she had not wanted to end the marriage. And that her husband had hurt her in ways she had never expected and would probably never recover from. Garrison remembered pulling out a chair for Reyna. He also remembered her flinching from him. Her reaction had hurt, twisted him with guilt even though he knew he'd done nothing wrong. At least not technically.

In hindsight, Garrison should have insisted that Barbieri provide for her, even though she had pressed for nothing on her own behalf and seemed to be waiting on the man she'd spent nearly half her life with to treat her fairly. Garrison's inaction, and Reyna's sadness, had haunted him ever since.

But the Reyna who had confronted him outside the bathroom was not the same sad woman he'd met five years before. Not at all. This Reyna Barbieri was stunning for a completely different reason.

She wore her confidence like a royal cloak. And her snapping black eyes had challenged him the moment she realized who he was. Her shoulder-length curls were tight and thick, inviting him to sink his hands into them and pull her closer. And her body. Christ Almighty…

The long and tight sweater hugged a figure that came straight from his dreams, a slender but curvaceous body he could easily imagine taking into his arms and making love to all night. Because of her, he was powerfully aware of every masculine part of him, aware that he wanted to be intimately joined to every feminine part of her.

Ignoring his work, Garrison stroked his lower lip

Chapter 3

By the time she got back to her seat, Reyna's heart was beating way too fast, as if she'd just finished a marathon. Her cheeks felt flushed, and she was fighting the urge to look back over her shoulder at Garrison. What was wrong with her?

"You all right, girl?" Louisa, the most perceptive of all her friends, asked as she sat down.

The women had taken out a deck of cards, and Bridget was dealing.

"Yeah. I'm good." She forced a smile and cleared her throat. "What did I miss?"

Louisa gave her a concerned glance but didn't press it. "We're playing blackjack. The winner gets a massage at the resort."

"I could definitely use one of those." She lifted her tight shoulders with a sigh of anticipation. "Prepare to lose your shirts, ladies!" Reyna pushed her encounter with her ex's lawyer to the back of her mind and focused on the card game.

An hour later, the train arrived at their stop. Although she hated that she was paying attention, Reyna noticed Garrison getting off the train with her and her friends, immediately walking toward the taxi stand. She breathed a quiet sigh of relief and clambered from the train. Garrison wasn't going to the resort with them. She didn't have to worry about seeing him again.

Outside the climate-controlled train, the day was crisp and cold. The sun had cleared away the snowy clouds, covering the white-and-green landscape in warm gold. Reyna breathed a lungful of crisp mountain air. It felt good to be at Halcyon again.

"He's cute!" Bridget looked over her shoulder at Reyna as she followed Louisa and Marceline into the black SUV that the resort had sent for them.

Reyna gave her rolling duffel bag to the driver and claimed a seat by the window. "Who?"

Louisa made a disbelieving sound. "The guy you've been staring at for the past five minutes."

Reyna blushed and turned her attention to the window as the Range Rover powered through the snow and up the hill toward the ski resort. Bridget and Louisa laughed while Marceline gave her a reassuring smile.

"He is a cutie," her friend said. "There's nothing wrong with looking."

Reyna clenched her back teeth but didn't say anything.

It was a gorgeous morning in the Adirondack Mountains. With the windows up, the heater on and the driver playing a lively Beyoncé song, the women were comfortably isolated from the outside chill. Reyna sighed and relaxed into the heated seats, ignoring Bridget and Louisa's chatter. The SUV growled up the path toward Halcyon Ski and Mountain Resort, a sprawling circle of cabins on a hilltop that overlooked majestic mountains and wintry fields of white.

In Halcyon, the air was crisp and sharp, a welcome change from what Reyna experienced every day in the city. With the company of her girls, being there always made her feel refreshed, even if she was in one of her bad moods.

The resort was one of the lesser-patronized places of the "it" crowd that Bridget and Louisa knew. It was beautiful, exclusive and scenic, with just about every amenity available. And it was a place people came to for the privacy as much as they did for the skiing.

Halcyon was the one truly big splurge Reyna allowed herself every year. The resort had become the place for her to get away from all the things worrying her in the city. Her career at the tattoo parlor where she'd worked since her divorce, the MFA degree in Graphic Design she'd gotten during her marriage but never used, the decision of what graphic arts jobs to apply for, *if* she did take the plunge.

Working at the tattoo parlor was fun, but every day she felt more and more like the only girl in a college fraternity. The boys who worked there—although over twenty-five—were all about picking up women, going to bars and getting more ink on their bodies. She'd outgrown the place a long time ago but was nervous about making the necessary change.

"God! This place gets more and more beautiful

every year." Louisa sighed as they drove past a grove of naked trees. Their barks were a dark brown against the white landscape, branches covered in snow and stretched out above them like lace.

Reyna agreed with a silent nod, staring out her own window.

"Hopefully there'll be hotter guys up here this year," Bridget said as she freshened up her bright lipstick with the help of her compact. "Last year was a bust." She pressed her lips together then snapped the compact shut.

A woman who always did whatever she wanted, Bridget was more than willing to have a fling at the resort and never look back after the weekend. Reyna could never do that. Sleeping with a man at the place that had become her sanctuary from drama just seemed like a very, very bad idea.

"I hear that Ahmed Clark might be up here this year." Marceline shared the information with the slightest of smiles.

At one time or another, the women had all drooled over the rising basketball star. Unlike his teammates, who they all thought were freakishly tall or had too many tattoos, Ahmed was just perfect. He was six and a half feet tall, wore a wide and frequent grin while on the basketball court and regularly gave money and time to charity. His body wasn't half-bad, either.

Bridget chuckled. "I guess I know who I'll be hooking up with this weekend." She pouted her freshly reddened lips and winked.

"*If* rumors are reliable." Louisa raised a skeptical eyebrow.

"If he's up at Halcyon, that man will be under me before the weekend is through," Bridget said.

Reyna laughed and shook her head at her friend. If only Bridget was that relentless about figuring out her life, she wouldn't still be living at her parents' place and steadily burning through her trust fund.

"Honey, why do you have to make this weekend about sex?" Marceline looked as if she was only partially joking. "It's supposed to be about us, remember? You and your girls."

"Yes, but you girls like to sleep, and I don't. I have to fill the time somehow." Bridget gave Marceline a saucy wink then started fiddling with her phone.

They arrived at the resort a few minutes later. The lodge where they would check in, eat, drink and socialize was a big and beautiful old-fashioned log cabin straight out of a mountain woman's dream. The two-story lodge contained a restaurant upstairs and the shop and front desk downstairs. The restaurant's wide glass windows overlooked a dizzying view of the mountains.

Far back and behind the lodge, although they couldn't be seen from the main path, sat over two dozen log cabins, each with two to four bedrooms, a fireplace, wireless internet and a kitchen in case anyone was intrepid enough to cook.

After Reyna and her friends checked in at the front desk, another driver chauffeured them in a covered golf cart down the snowy path to their cabin. They tumbled into the heated cabin, stretching and groaning from the long morning of sitting on the train and then in the SUV. The driver dropped their bags, com-

plete with ski equipment, by the front door before
quietly leaving with his tip.

"This isn't our usual cabin." Bridget looked around,
hands on her hips.

"You're just now noticing that?" Louisa grabbed
her bag and walked toward one of the bedrooms.

"It's fine, Bridg." Reyna patted her friend's shoulder and headed for the other bedroom. "There aren't
any bad cabins up here anyway."

The frown didn't leave Bridget's face when she
followed Reyna into the room. But she quickly forgot her dissatisfaction when Louisa appeared in their
doorway wearing a teal ski suit, complete with furred
hat and boots. Very black Russian sex kitten.

Louisa posed in the middle of the bedroom.
"Who's ready to go check out the place?"

"That's not fair!" Bridget said, eyeing Louisa's
clinging and questionably warm outfit. "I want to
be sexy, too."

Reyna groaned. "Then change already. There's
a glass of hot apple cider waiting out there for me."

After Bridget got sexed up to her satisfaction, the
four women made their way to the lodge. As their
booted feet crunched through the snow, Bridget
teased Marceline out of her funk while Reyna and
Louisa walked behind them.

"So who was that guy you were checking out on
the train?" Louisa asked.

She kept her voice low, but at a conversational level
so the other women wouldn't think she was trying to
hide anything from them.

Reyna shrugged. Lying about Garrison Richards's
identity would be a waste of time. Louisa was smart

and had a husband named Google. If those resources failed, her brother worked high up in the FBI and could get her any information she wanted. Sometimes she was a little scary.

"He's someone I knew years ago," Reyna finally said. "From the divorce."

"Ah." Louisa grinned, her eyes sparkling as if she'd just found out a secret. "That explains why you didn't look exactly glad to see him." She squeezed Reyna's waist. "But you couldn't look away from him, either. I don't blame you. He's a sexy beast." She growled playfully.

Reyna paused, surprised that Louisa didn't throw around any of her usual adjectives for people she found appealing: hot, handsome, fine. Maybe because Garrison was none of those things. He was too stern, too cold, to be anything but sexy. And a beast. She swallowed thickly at the thought.

While in that conference room with him five years ago, she hadn't paid any attention to his looks. He had been all shark, cool and efficient. Presenting her with the facts of her impending divorce after drafting the awful document that allowed her ex-husband to toss her out on the streets with nothing. Admittedly, she had been young and foolish, naively relying on Ian to do the right thing.

Reyna sighed. "Yes. He is sexy. If you like that sort of thing."

"*That sort of thing?* Girl…" Louisa chuckled. "What man-loving woman with a working libido wouldn't be into *that sort of thing*?" She fanned her face and grinned.

Reyna had to silently agree. Garrison's understated

dress only emphasized the belly-quivering masculinity of him. The subtle swagger in his walk, the way he appeared to see clearly everything around him. Those small details made her wonder wicked things. Like what kind of focus he would have in bed. Would he please his woman first and take his own pleasure at the end of a long and sweat-dripped night? How would it feel when his…? She cleared her painfully dry throat.

The fur on Louisa's hooded jacket fluttered around her face as she laughed. "You don't fool me one little bit, honey."

At the lodge, they found their usual table near the window and beneath one of the heater vents. Unwilling to wait for table service, Bridget went to get them a round of hot apple cider. Reyna stretched her legs under the table next to Marceline's, more than ready for the relaxing weekend.

The lodge's restaurant, which could comfortably hold at least fifty people, was already a quarter full on that Friday morning. Conversation wound through the airy space, mixing with laughter and the clink of cups and saucers. The guests were a mix of couples, singles and groups all gathered at their tables to enjoy the morning and the beginning of the weekend.

"Here you go, ladies." Bridget came back to the table with a silver kettle and four matching cups on a tray. "The first round is on me."

A collective sigh of appreciation went around the table. At first, Reyna thought it was for the apple cider, then she noticed that none of the women were paying any attention to the drink. Instead, their gazes were fastened on something over her shoulder. Ahmed Clark, Reyna guessed without looking. But she was wrong. Instead of the basketball player, it was Garrison Richards who had walked through the door.

She drew a breath of surprise. What was he doing here? She thought he had… Reyna shook her head. It didn't matter. All she knew was that her friends were acting like hormonal teenagers.

She wanted to slap them all. But while pouring a glass of cider for herself, she snuck a look at Garrison from under her lashes. Yes, he was sexy. There was no denying that. There was also no denying that she should stay away from him. It took a ridiculously long time for her friends to stop staring at him like vultures at the sight of new carrion.

Louisa poured drinks for the rest of the women and slid Reyna a private, provoking glance. "He's a nice specimen," she said to Marceline. "Maybe that's just what you need to get over your broken heart this weekend."

"I'm pretty sure Reyna has dibs on him already." Marceline's voice seemed tinged with regret.

"Hmm," Bridget chimed in. "He is a cutie! Isn't that the guy from the train?"

"Most definitely." Louisa grinned. "And I don't see a ring."

She was the most perceptive of them all, but was also the most cruel, using her insight to play games that most people were not ready for. Louisa gave Reyna another annoying look, but Reyna didn't bite. She only shrugged and tasted her cider. It was perfect, the heated cinnamon, sugar and apples coating her tongue with delicious flavor. Just the perfect thing on such a cool and spectacularly beautiful day.

Reyna kept her eyes on the cider and not on the man her friends refused to stop staring at.

"You know that a ring doesn't mean much these days," Bridget said, picking up from Louisa's earlier comment. "Some married men travel without theirs just to pick up some stranger before going back home to the wife." Bridget nodded in Garrison's direction, although he was far from the only man in the lodge. Reyna was willing to bet, though, that he was the most…appealing. With the gray heads, men who were obviously with their lovers and the immature-looking boys, Garrison was unfortunately the hottest thing in the room.

"Yeah, what's that about?" Marceline muttered. "I know plenty of girls who would love to land a married man. If he had on a wedding ring, it'd be like catnip."

"Maybe they don't realize exactly what they're trolling for," Bridget said. "Territorial women can be vicious."

Louisa gestured with her cup. "That's not the only thing they have to watch out for. Some of these hot-ass married men have diseases they're ready to pass on to anyone, including their wives."

A chorus of agreement went around the table.

While the women got distracted from Garrison with the talk of cheating married men, Reyna watched him from the corner of her eye. So she noticed that he sat at the empty seat closest to the fire, his booted feet nearly nudging the grate. And she also noticed when he started watching her.

He took a sip of his drink and looked at her over the edge of his cup. She ducked her head, but not before his penetrating gaze managed to scatter her senses.

She came in on the tail end of her friends' conversation about cheating. "I don't know why anyone would want to have an affair with a married man. Seems like a recipe for heartache to me. And not just for the actual wife whose husband is doing the messing around." She knew from experience how awful that was. "These girls might get attached and then fool themselves into thinking their lovers are going to leave their wives." Ian had been cheating on her, but as far as she knew, he never married or lived with any of the women he'd cheated with.

"Some women just like to gamble." Louisa shrugged.

"Pardon my intrusion, ladies."

They all looked up. Reyna's fingers twitched around her cup of cider, and she had to clutch it tighter to stop from accidentally spilling it.

Garrison stood near their table. He seemed perfectly at ease in his thick gray sweater and jeans. And by *at ease*, Reyna's mind supplied, she meant *sexy as hell*. He stood with a hand in his pocket, his gaze trained firmly on her.

"I'm Garrison Richards." He looked at all the women before bringing his eyes back to Reyna. "I want to apologize to Ms. Barbieri—"

"I don't go by that name anymore," Reyna interrupted. "It's Allen now."

"My apologies." He dipped his head. A spark of something flared in his eyes, but his face remained cool. "But please allow me to apologize again when I didn't recognize you earlier."

"No apologies necessary," she said. "It's been five years, and we only met a couple of times."

"You are quite unforgettable," he said.

His hawkish gaze tightened something low in her belly. She swallowed and tried to ignore it.

"I'm frankly surprised," Reyna said. "You must have been through hundreds of women like me."

She felt the shocked gazes of her friends. They knew it wasn't like her to be so rude.

But Garrison wasn't fazed. "I doubt there's anyone like you." A small, unamused smile touched his mouth. "I'd like to invite you to dinner one night this weekend, if I may?" He pulled a card from his wallet and held it out to Reyna. A calling card, she noticed, one without his business information.

When she didn't take it, he put it on the table in front of her. "You don't have to give me your answer now, but be sure to call me when you decide to accept." After another nod at Reyna and her friends, he turned and headed back to his table.

Marceline and Bridget stared at her with their mouths hanging open. Louisa only smiled. Like the Cheshire Cat, she sipped from her glass of cider and waited for what Reyna had to say.

"You have to tell us where you know that fine-ass guy from!" Bridget aimed a far from subtle gaze at Garrison's table. "Oh, my God! I bet he's tasty."

The sadness in Marceline's face receded with her curiosity. "Yes, fess up. Our not-so-little Reyna has been keeping secrets."

She tried not to wince at the reference to her

height, something she had always been self-conscious about. Instead, she shrugged.

"He is someone I met—"

A ripple went through the lodge just then.

"It's Ahmed!"

Her friends all turned toward the door. Ahmed Clark had walked into the room and given Reyna a temporary reprieve. She wasn't ready yet to tell her friends how she met Garrison.

It was not that she was ashamed of it. But that was a time in her life filled with such pain and betrayal that she'd rather not revisit it. They all knew the pertinent details of the divorce and what happened afterward. They had been there for her when she found out Ian had been sleeping around, when she confronted him, when he demanded a divorce, telling her she wasn't the kind of wife a TV star like him should have.

It seemed so ridiculous at the time. So surreal. The boy she had known in high school, pimply faced and gangly. The one whom no other girl had paid the slightest bit of attention to, but had been her friend, then lover, then husband. They had blossomed from their teenaged awkwardness together, Ian becoming more beautiful than anyone had ever imagined, the swan in his duckling family.

He'd never seriously considered acting, but when an uncle in the business suggested that he try out for a TV role, Ian dived in and never looked back.

Dismissing the past, Reyna turned with her friends to watch Ahmed Clark stroll into the restaurant with a tall beauty at his side. He was pretty enough to be a movie star himself. So was the woman with him.

"Damn, he's fine!" Bridget made a show of licking her lips and moaning his name. "Give me five minutes, Ahmed, and I'll make you forget all about that skinny red bone on your hip."

Reyna chuckled. She didn't doubt that her friend's boast could come true. Bridget was beautiful and determined enough. Across the table from her, Louisa picked up Garrison's card and tucked it into her pocket. Her smile was pure mischief.

After another round of hot cider, Reyna and the girls left the lodge and took the ski lift to the top of the mountain. In the glass-and-steel lift, Reyna marveled at the lush spread of the Adirondacks beneath and around them. New York City was incredible, and Reyna couldn't imagine living anywhere else. But she loved the wildness of the mountains, its fierce beauty, the evergreens drooping with the cold, white weight of the snow.

Once at the top of the mountain, her friends hit the slopes on their skis and left Reyna to her own devices. Around her, children played with snowballs and with each other, giggling and rolling down the abbreviated slope. Couples and groups hiked up the hill, the sound of their conversations floating back down to Reyna as she watched her friends, one after the other, disappear down the ski slope.

"See you at the bottom!" Bridget flashed a brilliant white smile and took off after the others.

Boots planted firmly in the snow, Reyna waved her off.

She didn't ski. After a disastrous lesson a few years ago that ended with a broken wrist, she gave up trying to learn. But that didn't mean she enjoyed their annual ski retreat any less. She just got her pleasure a different way.

She climbed carefully through the snow and over the craggy rocks toward an even better view of the slopes and Halcyon's lodge and cabins at the bottom of the mountain. As she climbed, she left more and more people behind. Her footsteps dragged through the thick snow, and her every breath misted the air.

Reyna was breathing hard when she finally found the perfect place to sit—a jutting dark rock she brushed the snow from to settle into the dip made perfectly for her butt. She was slightly breathless and warm under her clothes. Even her daily trek through New York streets had not prepared her for the im-promptu hike.

From her perch out in the open, she watched the anonymous bodies whipping down the slopes and through the snowy fields far below. Their whoops of joy broke into the air like the sound of champagne, happy and celebratory. The sun reflected brightly off the field of white and into her eyes shielded by dark glasses. It was a gorgeous day.

Reyna took off her hat to better feel the bright sun on her head. She took a sketchbook and pencil from her backpack and pulled off her right glove. The air was cold, but bearable on her fingers as she began to sketch. Soon, she lost herself in the movement of her pencil across the page, the sweeping and scratching rhythm of it as she captured the mountain on paper. A blurred shape flew past her, whipping the nearby snow-laden spruce in its breeze. She lifted her head.

A snowboarder. Tall and graceful, dressed in head-to-toe gray. He whipped past her, a contained storm. And it had to be a he, with his very masculine silhouette and the aggressive way he took the mountain. Flecks of snow flew up under his board. Reyna watched as he soared off the mountain and hung in the air for a moment, one hand gripping the side of the board, the other outstretched. He was a dark outline in the bright landscape, a wild and beautiful thing, before landing once again among the white then disappearing around a bend in the mountain and from her sight.

A few more lightning-quick shapes whipped past her, each in brightly colored clothes that made them stand out against the snow, but it was the man in gray who caught and held her attention. The other snowboarders zipped down the mountain, as exuberant as children, calling out to each other, shouting in masculine camaraderie.

Distracted from her sketches, she searched for the man in gray. *Ah, there he is.* She followed his somber presence down the mountain, the way he sliced across the snow, beautiful and untouchable.

Before she was aware of what she was doing, Reyna began to sketch him, the sharp grace of him racing down the mountain, knees bent, arms outstretched as if he was flying, his entire face covered up. She lost herself in the rhythm of sketching, the world as she saw it coming to life under her fingers. Long minutes passed.

"Aren't your fingers cold?"

Reyna stiffened at the sound of the shouted question. It was Garrison Richards. Again.

"No," she said. "They're fine."

But she put down her pencil—her hand *was* actually damn near frozen—and curled it in her lap. Only a few feet away, Garrison was slowly skimming down the hill toward her...on a *snowboard*? Her mouth fell open.

If she wasn't seeing him with her own eyes, she would have thought a sport like snowboarding completely unlike him. He seemed best suited for cold and emotionless things like chess, polo or even rowing. Not this howling and graceful sport that was all adrenaline, physical power and falling down in the snow. She couldn't even see him falling, being messy and human enough to tumble and get up and try something again. She imagined that he always did everything right the first time.

Garrison had pulled his gray ski mask from over his mouth, revealing full lips and that unexpected dimple in his chin. His goggles reflected twin images of her sitting on the dark rock with her mouth open.

She snapped her teeth together with a sharp click.

Garrison turned skillfully on the board and stopped near her. He was dressed completely in gray. Gray? She did a double-take and glanced down the hill toward the man she had been sketching. He wasn't there. She had a sinking feeling that he was the one at her side. He must have taken the lift back up and circled around.

Garrison clicked his feet from the latches on the snowboard. He was slightly out of breath, his lips parted to blow trailing heat into the air.

"I feel cold just looking at you." He started to pull off his gloves. "Take these. Your friends would be very disappointed if you came back to the ski lodge with some fingers missing from frostbite."

She shook her head and picked up the thick pair of snow gloves next to her. "I already have some." She pulled on the gloves, wincing as her fingers burned from the cold.

Garrison resituated his gloves on his hands. He watched her, his face expressionless. No smile, merely his eyes hungrily moving over her, like a visual devouring. It left her with a strange feeling, that voracious gaze. Not unpleasant…but not exactly warm and fuzzy, either.

She stared back at him, refusing to look away.

They were hardly alone. Occasional skiers and snowboarders blew past them, whipping up snow and stirring up the cold in the air. But it felt as if they were isolated together on the mountain with only the sky and sun to look down on them. She didn't want to feel that with him. Reyna deliberately turned away from Garrison. "What do you want?"

"You didn't use my business card yet."

"I'm not going to."

Snow crunched, and the air moved as he came closer to her. Over the crispness of the pine trees and the cool bite of the snow, she smelled him. Sweat and a faintly woodsy cologne. The tang of sunblock. His gray jacket brushed her bright yellow one when he sat next to her. Although she knew it was impossible, it felt as if their skin touched.

"So, be honest." There was amusement in his voice, although his face did not change. "Do you plan on hating me forever, Ms. Allen?"

"I don't hate you."

She sat with him, unable to get even that simple fact out of her mind. She was sitting with Garrison Richards. The man who she perhaps may not have hated, but had strong and poisonous feelings for. On that first day in his office, receiving the brunt of his cool and arrogant stare meant to unnerve her and make her give up everything else she had, she'd wanted nothing more than to rush from the conference room and out into the sun, letting it burn away the ice-cold bath that had been his gaze.

And now he was here with her in the snow. Under the burning sun, asking her about hating him forever. The world was a strange place.

"Isn't there some sort of ethical problem with you being here with me?" she asked.

"You are the wife of a former client. Ian Barbieri doesn't have me on retainer, and he and I have no business dealings. I see no conflict of interest here. But I can check if that makes you feel any better." She heard the smile in his voice again. *Bastard.*

The only real conflict was probably in her. She remembered the past much too vividly and irrationally blamed him for what happened to her during the divorce. More so than even her ex-husband.

Reyna squirmed at that uncomfortable realization.

She wanted to get back to her sketching, but her hand hurt too much from the cold. She must have made some motion toward her sketch pad because Garrison looked over at it. Too late, she remembered that she had been working on a sketch of the snowboarder—of him!—just before he sat down. She didn't justify his curiosity by trying to hide her work.

He took off his thick gloves, revealing thin black

leather that clung to his fingers like a second skin. His hands were big, she noticed, but graceful.

"May I?"

She clenched her teeth against refusing him. Maybe the sooner he saw what she was doing, the sooner he would leave. His fascination with her was... distracting. She ignored the rational part of her that chimed in about her own unwanted fascination with the ruthless lawyer.

"Sure," she said in response to his question. "Just don't get my stuff wet." Reyna froze and almost bit her tongue off at what she just said.

He arched a dark, slashing eyebrow. "I think that's the first time I've ever had a woman say that to me."

She stared at him in shock. But he was reaching for her sketch pad, and his austere grace seemed even more so beneath the brilliance of the early-afternoon sunlight. Except for the reflective goggles crowning his head, he could have been in any boardroom in the world. Removed and critical. His powerful hands carefully handled her sketchbook, flipping through its pages, pausing at one or two before moving on. Yes, definitely critical.

"These sketches are wonderful." He flipped another page of the book, going from the images of the snowboarder she'd captured more thoroughly, to her earlier on-the-fly doodles of the mountain, the snow, the dots of people winding below her toward the lodges. "You're very talented."

"Thank you." She hid her surprise at his unexpected compliment, not quite knowing what else to say in response. If this was part of his campaign to satisfy his strange curiosity about her, he was choosing the wrong way to go about it. She didn't respond well to insincerity.

But a brief look from his hawkish eyes made her realize that this wasn't a man who said something he didn't mean. An unwelcome warmth began to unfurl in her belly. Reyna hissed quietly and braced her gloved hands against the rock, glad for the dull pain that distracted her from his compliments, his nearness.

This was Garrison Richards, she reminded herself. Again.

"My mother draws, too," he continued in his low and compelling voice. "And don't tell her I said this, but your work is much more interesting, more fluid." He flipped back to the sketch of the snowboarder. Of himself. "I admire the way you capture the image in a personal way. You're there with the subject instead of just watching. The intimacy is very seductive."

Was he playing with her? Didn't he know he was talking about himself? But he turned to the sketches of the mountain that she'd begun to fill in with long strokes of the pencil. Craggy slopes, white snow, a feathering of trees. The wide and low-hanging sky that kissed the mountaintop just so. "It's like you're a nature sprite sitting in the cloud here." He tapped the page at a cloud she had half drawn. "Watching this world that you love."

Heat touched her cheeks at his suggestive and unexpected comments. She didn't know what to say, so she didn't say anything.

She looked away from the sketchbook in Garrison's hands, the white paper held between fingers that were an odd mix of rugged and refined. They were almost a working man's hands, but the way he handled her work, even through the thin leather gloves, was like a curator touching something delicate and easily damaged. A contradiction she didn't want to notice but was helpless not to. It made him even more interesting than she had first thought. Now he was more than his dangerously sexy looks, more than the unpleasant history between them. She forced her gaze away from his hands.

"It's just a hobby," she said finally, training her eyes on the vast mountain view spread out before her. The thick clouds tumbling through the skies promised another bout of snow.

"Somehow I doubt that. Talent like this has to be more than a hobby." He nodded toward the sketch pad. "Do you do this for a living?"

She flinched when Garrison carefully replaced the sketch pad on the rock next to her. Reyna smelled him as he leaned behind her, the tang of his aftershave, sweat and sunscreen overwhelming her senses. She closed her eyes briefly to savor the scent of him, then snapped them open when she realized what she was doing.

What did he just ask her? She drew a steadying breath. "I'm a tattoo artist, so I guess I do. People occasionally ask me to do original sketches and portraits for their body art."

"Really?" He glanced over her body as if he could see under her clothes to any ink she may or may not have beneath them. "Tattoos?"

"Yes. Tattoos." Reyna stiffened, preparing for another of Garrison's judgmental looks.

She rarely told people what she did for a living.

Unless they came into the studio where she worked, people never assumed Reyna was any more than she appeared: a slightly boring, nice girl. Not that being a tattoo artist exempted her from being boring. Once people found out her job, men in particular, they only wanted to know one thing. Or maybe two. And they always assumed she had some hidden pain kink or was a bad girl looking for a bad boy.

"How unique," Garrison said. "I'm sure your work is some of the most beautiful in the city."

She warmed again at his compliment. And at his unexpected reaction to her job. It was such a very different reaction from the one she'd gotten from her ex-husband, someone who had known her for most of her adult life. With Garrison's thoughtful silence, she drifted into the past to the one and only time she'd been in the same place with Ian after the divorce.

One night, he had wandered into her tattoo studio from off the busy nighttime street. Reyna was in her zone, the buzz of the needle vibrating between her fingers as she sat on a chair working on the large trail of red poppies a pale-skinned client wanted down her spine.

The bell above the door rang, announcing that someone had walked in, but she didn't pay much attention since she was already occupied. A hum of excitement began in the shop. Then she heard Ian's voice and couldn't stop herself from freezing up in automatic rejection of him being in her space.

He walked in like a big TV star, attracting the attention of everyone in the shop, signing autographs and pretending not to see her. But eventually, he hadn't been able to help himself and walked over to her sectioned-off area.

Ian jerked his chin in her direction. "I bet you're into bondage and all kinds of sick garbage now. You want a man to tie you up and make you bleed?"

Reyna continued her work, even when she felt her client's body tense with interest at Ian's proximity. She'd had months of practice keeping herself centered and calm. He drifted into her field of vision, but she acted as if he wasn't there.

Among other things, he called her a pain slut, ready for torture and blood at the hands of a lover. She focused on the tattoo gun in her hand, the red poppies taking shape beneath the needle.

Her nonresponsiveness worked perfectly. He never came by the studio again.

Reyna returned from her reverie to find Garrison watching her closely with his usual unreadable expression.

"Tattooing is not my passion," she said for want of some sort of barrier between them. "But it's an amazing thing to walk around the city sometimes and see a client with my work on their body."

"I can only imagine how satisfying that would be." Garrison looked down the mountain, and Reyna followed his gaze.

Snow and fresh powder, nothing but cold white for miles. His hobby, or passion. Another surprise between them.

"You should go," she said. "Don't waste this. It won't last long."

She didn't know if she was talking about the snow or the weekend or life.

"You're right," Garrison said. "Nothing really lasts, does it?" His intent eyes settled on her again. "All the more reason to enjoy it while you can instead of looking ahead to its end."

Her mouth curled into a smile. "You can think of it that way, yes."

He nodded as if he'd decided something. "I'll be seeing you again, Ms. Allen."

She watched him click back onto his snowboard, pull on his thick gloves and mask and lower his goggles. He seemed alien and untouchable against the landscape that was all sunlight, the cheerful dip of the evergreens, a clear blue sky. All around she heard the joyful shouts of people enjoying themselves in the snow.

"Until then." She dipped her head in his direction.

He scudded down the mountain, kicking up snow in his wake, the movement of his dark shape on the bright snow pulling an aching cord in her belly. She drew in a breath at the warm feeling. No. She did not want this.

It was one thing to find him attractive. It was another entirely to find herself actually *attracted* to him. The subtle humor in his long-lashed eyes. His masculine scent. The fact that he wasn't as boring and arrogant as she expected. Reyna swallowed thickly, and she watched him fly away from her. She had a feeling she was about to get herself in trouble.

Reyna spent another couple of hours sketching and enjoying her semi-isolation before her friends came back and dragged her from her mountain perch for sledding and impromptu drinks with some men they'd met on the slopes. Ahmed Clark was not among these eligible bachelors, but Bridget was happy enough.

Later on, in the cabin and under the influence of the hot toddies Louisa made, her friends tried to go back to the subject of Garrison Richards. But Reyna steered them toward something else. Louisa smirked, her look telling Reyna that she couldn't avoid her feelings for the lawyer, or her discussion of them, for too much longer. But whatever respite she had, Reyna would gladly take. Garrison made her feel too uneasy, overheated and uncomfortable for her to talk about him just yet. Even to her closest friends.

They stayed up until late, talking about life and love and everything in between. At a little past three in the morning, the women all pled exhaustion, even Bridget. Reyna, however, was still wide awake. She didn't need much sleep, and working at the tattoo studio, which was open until 4:00 a.m. some Saturdays, she was used to going to bed as late as six in the morning.

After her friends went to bed, she couldn't slow down her mind. She couldn't stop thinking about Garrison and his snow-flecked flight down the mountain. She couldn't stop thinking about his *smell*. Spicy and masculine, like a long and back-bending night in a warm bed.

It was as if he was still next to her, body crowding her on the couch, inflaming her late-night imagination with thoughts of what it would be like to kiss him. Wondering what harm there would be to allow him this chase at the resort, allow him to catch her and be with her away from real life in the city.

The more her body marinated in thoughts of having him, the more her brain shouted at her to stop being so stupid. He wasn't a good person. He was just as bad as Ian, maybe worse.

Her thoughts grew clamorous, too loud and too shameful to be cooped up in the cabin with so many sleeping souls. She got up from the couch and dampened the fire, pulled on her snow gear and stepped out into the cold.

Chapter 4

Garrison sat in the armchair by the fire, shirtless and wearing jeans. His sock-covered feet were stretched out toward the fireplace. The heat from the flames flickered over his bare chest, warming and sweet.

At four in the morning, the snow was coming down outside, whirling in pale flurries against the dark sky. The fire burned hot and high behind the grate. The heater was on. It was nearly eighty degrees in the cabin, just how he liked it. The book he had started to read lay turned down on his thigh, but his mind was far from immersed in its chapters. Instead, his thoughts were full of Reyna.

Garrison had been surprised to see her on the trail earlier that day. It was as if he had been given a gift when he saw her sitting on that rock, removed from the chaos and rabble around her, a queen surveying her lands. He saw her as he came down the mountain then whipped past her on his board. A bubble of exquisite feeling popped to life inside him. It had overtaken the euphoria and freedom he usually felt from being on the mountain with the board under his feet. And he had damn near broken his neck to quickly get down the mountain then back up again to reintroduce himself.

And now, more than twelve hours later, he was still thinking about her. Reyna Allen. The artist. The woman.

Although he wasn't one for commitments—his career as a divorce attorney forced him to see the futility of those sorts of arrangements—there was something about Reyna that made him want her. Want her badly.

On the mountain, he had only just restrained himself from kissing her. Her lips, glistening and red from the ChapStick or lipstick or whatever she'd applied, distracted and tangled his thoughts. In her presence, all clarity disappeared. All he wanted to do was kiss her and sink his fingers into her hair and make her sigh his name. Even now, the thought of her mouth made the muscles in his belly tighten.

Garrison had never had a vacation hookup before, but the fire in Reyna's eyes made him want to try something new. A flicker of movement outside the window drew him from his thoughts. The brief flash of a woman's face under a yellow hooded jacket. Reyna.

Without giving himself a chance to think, Garrison quickly pulled on his cold-weather clothes and rushed out the door after her. His heart raced as the primitive side of him, long buried by an exacting and regimented life, rose up to follow Reyna as if she were *his* female, scented temptingly on the wind.

The door clicked shut behind him, and snow crunched under his boots. Pale flurries swirled around him in the brisk breeze, melting against his face. The cold night groaned with its particular noises.

Reyna walked slowly up ahead, hands in the pockets of her yellow jacket while the furred hood obscured most of her face and covered her head. He didn't try to be quiet. But he didn't call out to her, either. He quickly caught up with her, using his slightly longer legs to his advantage.

"Ms. Allen."

She turned, startled, her large black eyes widening even more. Dark curls tumbled into her face, and she took a step back.

"Are you following me?"

"Yes."

She looked surprised again. Then turned away from him to continue walking. Garrison took that as an invitation to fall in step with her. Reyna glanced at him.

"I don't want you following or stalking me," she said. "I had enough ruin from you to last a lifetime."

"Ruin?" He frowned. This wasn't the almost welcoming woman he'd talked with on the slopes earlier that afternoon. Reyna was acting as if that conversation between them never happened.

"Yes. Ruin." Her face grew harder, a beautiful mahogany mask under the falling snow. "Ian was not smart enough to think of all those conditions in the divorce papers by himself. It had to be you." Reyna's black eyes crackled with anger. There seemed to be some sort of fever burning inside her. She walked faster. "You helped him to leave me on the edge of desperation. After the divorce I had to start over completely."

Garrison nodded silently, feeling again the weight of the blame for how the Barbieri divorce had been settled. In hindsight, he should have never allowed Ian Barbieri to do the things he'd done to the woman he'd supposedly loved since high school. Reyna hadn't known what she was getting into. She hadn't even retained a lawyer of her own, for heaven's sake! But despite his attraction to her then, Garrison had been too caught up in his job, in the pure facts of the case, to do what was right.

"The divorce left me vulnerable and more alone than I'd ever been." She slowed her steps, and her harsh breaths steamed the air. Then she looked annoyed with herself that she'd told him that much.

Because of Reyna and her divorce, he'd become more human, more aware of the larger picture where both parties in the separation were concerned. Garrison was almost ashamed to admit that it had been because of his attraction to her that he'd even begun to second-guess the methods that had worked so well for him in the past. Shallow, but true. After Reyna, it was no longer about simply allowing his client to escape a previous romantic entanglement with the most money possible. It was about being fair.

"It wasn't my finest hour," he said finally. Inadequately. "And although it means nothing now, please allow me to apologize."

He'd spent untold weeks and months torturing himself with what he could have done to be fair to her five years ago. Then he dreamed about being the man to come to her rescue and save her from her marriage. Now he simply wanted to be the man in her bed.

He swallowed and fisted a gloved hand in his jacket pocket. The fierceness of his desire for her was almost frightening. Before he saw her on the train that morning, she had existed at the back of his mind as a sort of angel, inspiring him to be a better man. Now he wanted to pull her down in the dirt with him and kiss the innocence from her lips.

Reyna walked quietly by his side, thankfully oblivious to his yearning. She pushed the hood back from her face, and the snow fell on her hair, the white settling in her beautiful black curls. She tilted her face briefly up at the sky. Garrison watched a lucky snowflake melting against her lips. He watched, burning in his thirst, as those lips parted, and her tongue licked away the wet.

"Why apologize now?" she asked. "It's been five years."

"Because I didn't mean to hurt you then, and I don't want you to hold the past against me now." He paused. "And I want you to know that I'm not that man anymore."

"Why do you care what I think?"

"Isn't it obvious? I want to…woo you."

She made a disbelieving noise, the corner of her mouth tilting up. "Is that what they're calling it these days?"

Embarrassed heat rushed through him. Was it possible that she knew his thoughts? Did she know how badly he wanted to pull her down into the snow with him and beneath him? Beyond the pounding of his lustful heart, he could almost hear the sounds she would make, her sighs and moans and gasps of pleasure, while he lost himself in the heated clasp of her.

Garrison cleared his throat. "Yes, that's what I'd like to call it for now. *Wooing* is not such a bad word, is it?"

She looked at him again, and it was as if she could see into him, through him. "Wooing? Really?"

"Yes. Definitely," he said. "At least at first." Garrison allowed the humor to surface in his voice. And a hint of his desire.

Reyna made that same noise again but said nothing. She only kept walking while the snow fell in its silence around them, the quiet broken only by the sound of their footsteps in the white powder, the whisper of their breaths. Vapor streamed from her parted lips.

He looked away from her mouth, deliberately distracting himself from thoughts of how good it would feel wrapped... He clenched his fist hard enough to stretch the thin leather gloves beneath his thicker snow gauntlets. Desperately, he thought of other things.

At four in the morning, there was no one around but the two of them. Garrison could hear the far-off rumble of conversation perhaps near one of the outdoor hot tubs with a view of the mountains. From what his friend Wolfe had told him, people often used the cover of night to go skinny-dipping in the hot tubs, sit with the bubbling water up to their throats while the snow fell around them. That had little appeal for him.

He barely tolerated the snow as it was. A born and

bred Floridian, he'd only come to New York for college, then stayed after law school because he got a lucrative offer from a downtown firm. Fifteen years later, he was still in the city, but that didn't make him hate the snow and the cold any less.

At his side, Reyna held her face up to the sky. It was as if she'd forgotten he was there. She caught errant snowflakes on her tongue, her face a study in contentment while her lips glistened red with some sort of lip gloss. He wondered if she would taste sweet or spicy. Like strawberries or cinnamon.

He forced his mind back to where it belonged.

"I don't know how you can stand this weather," he said.

She glanced briefly at him. "Then you should go back to your cabin."

"Oh, no. I'm enjoying myself too much for that."

"I take it you're not the type of man who takes no for an answer, then?" She arched an eyebrow at him under the snow.

"Not in business. But I always listen when I hear it from a lady."

A doubting smile touched her red lips. "Do you?"

"Absolutely. I am thoroughly enjoying your company. But if you tell me to leave you alone, then I will."

She opened her mouth, perhaps to tell him just that, but then closed it without saying anything. Garrison walked with her for a few minutes in silence. He tracked her graceful steps, admiring the length of her legs even in the jeans that obviously had another layer underneath.

"Why are you up here anyway?" she asked.

"Shouldn't you be in the city ruining some other woman's life?"

He winced. "It doesn't quite work that way. And I have many women as clients."

"Then you're ruining some men's lives, too. Very equal opportunity of you."

Her words stung him more than he wanted to admit. Not just because they alluded to how much the divorce agreement had hurt her, but also because she clearly thought he hadn't changed.

"Contrary to what you think, ruining lives is not the business I'm in."

"I'll believe that when I see it."

They broke through the thick forest of trees and arrived at the edge of the mountain and the waist-high fence protecting them from the steep drop. Just then, the snowfall dwindled to almost nothing.

Garrison breathed a sigh of relief, hoping that meant the next day the skies would be clear. The white stuff was good enough for snowboarding. But he hated when it got into his eyes, freezing his face and turning to water on his headgear. His mother always laughed at that contradiction in him. A man who hated the snow but enjoyed snow sports.

Whenever she mentioned it, he would simply trot out his mantra of making the best of a bad situation. He believed in that saying. He lived by it.

He had little choice but to be in New York City for work, to make money. He had nothing except his mother and a few close friends in Florida. Since New York was the place he had to be, then he enjoyed what he could and otherwise stayed indoors with his heat on high.

Beyond the fence, the darkness-shrouded Adirondack Mountains lay spread out like a beautiful tapestry below him. It was a long way down. And the pessimist in him couldn't help but imagine the danger of falling from such a height, the mountain turning his flesh to mincemeat while he rolled down every scenic inch.

"God! This place is beautiful!" Reyna took in a deep breath of the night air. "I'm so blessed to come here every year."

Happiness lit up her face, her black eyes reflecting the paleness of the snow, her mouth lifted in a smile. Garrison wanted to kiss her. He wanted to feel those cool lips under his own and breathe in the happiness she felt. But he knew that wouldn't be welcomed. At least not yet.

Garrison took a step back from her. She turned from the stunning view to frown at him. "What?"

Her eyes were slightly tilted in her face, like a fox's. Her full mouth parted with her question and stayed temptingly open. Garrison gave up the tight rein on his control and reached for her. He drew in her startled breath and gave her back one of his own.

He trembled as if caught in her snowstorm. He felt cold and hot at once, needing the pressure of her body against his to ground him. Her mouth was cool on his, the soft petals of her lips still at first, then she pressed close to kiss him back. A sound of pleasured appreciation rumbled at the back of his throat, and he felt her sigh, her lips parting to give him the scorching inside of her mouth. She tasted sweet, like red apples and whiskey. Not spicy at all. Only heat and pleasure.

God...

Garrison pulled her closer, his body going rigid against hers, even separated by so many layers of clothes. He gripped her hips. Her mouth was hot and soft, her tongue a slow and sensuous stroke against his that stole his breath and made him want to take her immediately to bed. But the nearest bed was actually a snowbank, and the thought of coming to awareness from a lust-fueled tumble in the freezing snow was the only thing that stopped him from *begging* her to let him... Garrison shuddered.

Reyna's gloved hands curled into fists in the front of his jacket. Her breathing quickened. A mewling sound twisted from her throat and went straight to his groin. Maybe the snowbank wouldn't be so bad after all...

The noise of a twig snapping broke into Garrison's consciousness. Someone or something walking near. Reyna gasped and pulled away. Her fox eyes blinked and stared with accusation.

"What the hell are you *doing*?"

Her mouth was damp and swollen from their kisses. He tasted the flavor of her lip balm on his tongue and wanted more. Garrison barely stopped himself from pulling her close again.

"That was me showing you how much I'd like to *woo* you." His voice sounded deeper to his own ears, rumbling lower than its normal register.

"No!" Reyna backed away from him, her voice high in panic. "This *cannot* happen." Her harsh breath chuffed steam in the air.

A bitter-tasting disquiet coated Garrison's tongue. Had he done something she hadn't wanted? Had he hurt her? But he quickly remembered the returned

Chapter 5

Reyna woke to the sound of Bridget's gentle snores. The small clock on the bedside table told her it was barely ten o'clock. The thick window shades shielded her from the sun, but she could actually feel the lateness of the morning. She'd barely slept three hours.

She closed her eyes and moved restlessly in the bed. The reason for her mostly sleepless night floated beneath her eyelids. Garrison. She could almost feel the thrum of lust between them again. His mouth on hers. The commanding stroke of his tongue that melted her from the inside out. She remembered, shamefully, the way she had moaned his name under the night sky, ready to fall into the snow and allow him to do *anything* to her.

The passion had flared so readily between them that it made her breathless, caught completely off

guard. It had frightened her more than a little. Even
in her marriage, she'd never felt such a dreadful need
to be close to someone, to strip and lay herself bare
and devour, then be devoured in return. There was
no logic to the attraction.

This was *Garrison Richards*. The "tiger shark lawyer" of New York. Since her divorce, she'd run across
his name often enough in the papers and online to
know she hadn't been the only one to leave a meeting
with him feeling eviscerated and cast adrift.

Reyna stirred again under the sheets at the thought,
a dull ache throbbing in her belly. She was betraying
herself with every lustful thought she had of Garrison, continuing to swing the wrecking ball he had
taken to her life all those years ago. The ache in her
stomach sharpened, and she bit her lip until she tasted
blood. Next to her, Bridget drew in a breath. Her
snores stopped, and one eye flickered open.

"Is it time to get up already?" Bridget's voice was
rough with sleep.

"For some people, but we're on vacation so we can
sleep as late as we like."

But Bridget sat up and rubbed her eyes. She
reached up to make sure her sleeping cap was still in
place. "The slopes are calling."

She left the bed and disappeared into their shared
bathroom. Reyna snuggled into her pillow and slipped
back into her waking dream. The warmth from the
blankets easily lulled her back down into the sweetly
torturous cycle of desire, regret and self-flagellation
that the remembered kiss with Garrison evoked. She
groaned and squeezed her eyes tightly shut. Someone knocked on the door. Before she could invite

them in, the door popped open, and Louisa stood in the threshold.

"Come on, sleepyheads, the powder is gorgeous today."

"Can the non-skiers get a break?" she muttered, snuggling deeper into the sheets.

"No way! Marceline just finished making breakfast. Get yourself decent and come out to eat. You know the routine by now."

Reyna whined and covered her head. After four years of coming to the resort with her friends, the routine was one she was very familiar with: get up and get your butt out of bed or else. That didn't mean she had to like it.

But when Bridget left the bathroom smelling of toothpaste and mouthwash, Reyna pulled herself out of bed and got it together. The other women were already gathered around the kitchen table when she emerged from her room a few minutes later in her thick robe and slippers. She followed the smells of coffee and bacon to the only empty chair at the table. The room was loud with the sound of her friends' laughing voices. Even Marceline was in on the discussion about whether or not it was possible to actually die from an orgasm.

"Anyone who knows firsthand obviously isn't here to tell." Louisa laughed and reached for a slice of bacon from the platter at the center of the table.

"Oh, my God! I would die if my man croaked on me." Marceline braced her elbows on the table and had both hands wrapped around a steaming mug of coffee. Her hair was loose and tumbled around her face, lending her a relaxed, almost carefree air. "Can you imagine?"

"I don't have to imagine it," Bridget said. "Remember the time I dated that older guy, the chef from LA?"

The women laughed, all of them remembering exactly whom Bridget was talking about. She seemed to always have a man-related anecdote for every occasion.

"You didn't have any business dating that old man!" Louisa chortled. "Every time he saw you, he damn near had a heart attack. Your cleavage alone gave him palpitations."

Bridget grinned. "But he made such heavenly food and had the most talented hands. It seemed a shame not to try him out all the way."

"Then you almost put him in the grave," Reyna said. She poured herself a cup of coffee from the pot already on the table.

"Hmm! Almost is not the same thing as doing." Bridget laughed, her eyes crinkling at the corners.

She tucked her legs under her at the table and cracked a piece of bacon with her fingertips, looking more like a mischievous child than the grown progeny of adoring multibillionaires.

"What about you, Reyna? I can't believe someone as pretty as you never had a thing with a sugar daddy."

Reyna shrugged under their sudden attention, suspecting that they had been talking about her before she came into the kitchen. "You all know everything there is to know about my love life. I don't have one." A sad truth. After her divorce, she'd dated a few times, but nothing that she'd allowed to become too serious.

"He's not exactly old, but what about that sexy guy from yesterday?" Louisa waved a business card under Reyna's nose. Garrison's. "He's definitely interested." Her lips quirked up. "You could do much worse than him for a vacay booty call."

"Mmm-hmm. That man's booty is too nice for you to turn down," Bridget teased Reyna over her shoulder. "Did you see how nicely he filled out those jeans?"

Reyna winced at the idea of Bridget checking out Garrison's butt. The woman's appetite knew no bounds, and it did something bad to Reyna's insides that her friend could potentially set her sights on the tempting lawyer. *Her* lawyer.

"Even if Reyna noticed his fineness, she's not going to tell us." Louisa grabbed a can of whipped cream from the fridge and squirted a swirl of it in her coffee. "She's as secretive as a nun about her sex life."

"A nun?" Marceline, a staunch Catholic, narrowed her gaze at Louisa. "Nuns don't have sex!"

Bridget giggled. "Not according to the movies I've seen."

"Okay, ladies. That's enough." Reyna threw up her hands. "Don't you have a ski day to get ready for?"

Louisa chuckled. "Can we at least finish our breakfast first, Sister Reyna?"

The other women laughed.

Once they were finished with their meal, Marceline and the others showered and got themselves ready for the slopes while Reyna gathered the things she would need for her day: a book, bathing suit, calf-length hooded parka and thick gloves.

An hour later, she waved goodbye to her friends, who were all sexy and sleek in their ski clothes, and headed to one of the resort's large outdoor hot tubs with a view of the mountains. She passed the spread-out cabins, some with smoke still piping from their chimneys, and nodded to the few people who passed her on the way to a late breakfast or the ski lift.

It was morning and prime skiing time. The best time for Reyna to be at the hot tub. Most people took advantage of one of the three massive, circular hot tubs after a long day on the slopes.

The day was cold, the snow from last night still scattered on the walkway and around the tubs. Reyna's boots crunched over the snow, and she enjoyed the sound of it, a lonely and lovely kind of music in each step. What the resort-goers called the "play area" was empty, just as she'd hoped. The pools were covered for the season, but the three hot tubs were already bubbling, their jets gurgling in the clear and bright morning.

Reyna settled her things around her, then she quickly stripped to her bikini and splashed into the tub. Heated water immediately embraced her up to her chin. She shivered with pleasure.

The sun pleasantly stroked her face with its heat while steam rose from the water around her. Directly in front of her was one of the most spectacular views in the world. The brilliant blue sky and the mountain range stretched out far into the horizon. Along the edge of the Halcyon property, the tall evergreens danced in the morning breeze.

Reyna sighed again and rested her head back

against the towel she had folded for just that purpose. The water soaked into her body, loosening her muscles and releasing the tension she'd been holding for weeks. But as she relaxed, it wasn't long before her mind drifted to the events of the night before and to Garrison.

When she'd run away from him, she had also been running away from herself. Or at least trying to. There were so many things wrong with her attraction for him. He was ruthless, cold. The type of man she'd always been contemptuous of, always putting business before everything else. Workaholic, conscienceless, boring, a hard-ass. But why was it that everything about him also made her burn?

"It looks like you're entertaining some serious thoughts."

Her eyes flew away from the mountains. Garrison— *damn him!*—stood nearby. He was dressed for another day of snowboarding in a new set of gray clothes that only emphasized his raw masculinity. Charcoal jacket and pants, black gloves and a thick gray hat pulled low over his ears. Mirrored sunglasses covered his eyes.

"Are you stalking me again?"

"Not at all. This time I got an invitation." His snow boots thudded dully on the concrete near her. He took off his sunglasses and hooked them in his jacket pocket.

Without asking, Reyna knew it was Louisa who'd told him where she was. She remembered her friend toying with Garrison's card, looking as if she was up to no good.

"Next time you should make sure the invitation is from me before you show up," she said coldly. But she couldn't ignore the excited beat of her heart at his presence.

"Were my kisses that awful last night, Reyna?" His voice was a low and rumbling tease with a hint of concern. And the sound of her name on his lips...

Reyna's face grew warm. His voice took her back to that moment of mouth-on-mouth bliss, his gloved hands branding her hips through her clothes, the cool brush of his nose when she'd tilted her head to kiss him even more deeply. It was impossible to forget how fresh he had tasted, like limes and a necessary drink of water. She licked her lips as if the taste of him still lay there.

The ghost of a smile touched his mouth, and he seemed relieved. "I'll take that as a no, then."

Reyna drew a quick breath. Garrison's words cut her more deeply than perhaps they should have. It was humiliating, but he could see straight through her to the woman who was weak enough to forgive what he had done to her just for a chance to writhe shamelessly under him for his pleasure, and hers. But she didn't want to be that woman. What he'd done was unforgivable. Despite what he said the night before, he had *not* changed, and she didn't need to make herself look any more desperate than she already felt.

She bit down hard on the inside of her lip. "Please don't make any assumptions where I'm concerned. Just because I'm having a supreme lack of judgment right now doesn't mean I'm going to sleep with you and pretend five years ago never happened."

The hint of a smile fell from his face. "I wouldn't want you to pretend with me, Reyna."

She couldn't suppress the bone-deep quiver at the way his tongue curled again around her name.

"The past can't be erased," he continued. "I know that. But I want us to work through it and put it behind us. I want you in my bed."

She shook her head, mouth dry, feelings conflicted. She should jump up and tell him no again, tell him to leave her alone. But the words wouldn't come.

Garrison dragged a lawn chair closer to the tub and, heedless of the scattered snow on the piece of furniture, sat down. She flushed, realizing that he could see straight into the water to the bikini she wore. Not that she was ashamed of her body, but the intimacy of it and the heat in his gaze made her want to cover herself. Under the water, her nipples grew hard. She shifted her thighs beneath his lazy regard but refused to look away from him. He was the one intruding, after all.

"Garrison, please," she finally said. But she didn't know exactly what she was pleading for.

He seemed to sense the confusion in her, not pressing for an explanation, only waiting, watching. She was the one who broke first.

"I came out here to relax. Not to argue or fend off—" she couldn't bring herself to say *unwanted* "—advances. This is my vacation."

He nodded, a single dip of his dimpled chin. "Perfect. We both agree that this is a vacation, not combat." The chair sighed with his weight. His lashes flickered when he looked away from her to the almost painful blue of the sky. "Truce?"

Reyna bit her lip. "Truce."

"Good." His eyes didn't stay away from her for

very long. "Why aren't you on the mountain with the rest of them?"

Reyna blew out a breath of calming air. This was how they were going to play it? Okay. She could play along with the best of them. "Why aren't *you*? I hear it's perfect powder today."

"It is." He nodded and threw a glance upward to the snowy peaks above the resort. "But I had a few things to sort out for work this morning."

"Ah, a workaholic."

"No. A pragmatist. If I deal with this now, then I can ease into my day on Monday."

"So a pragmatist *and* a workaholic, then," she said.

"Do you have an issue with workaholics?"

"Not at all. It just means that you're no fun." *Damn.* Was she actually flirting with him?

He raised an eyebrow. "I've never had any complaints about my level of fun." His eyes dipped again to her body in the water. "Speaking of complaints, I have none regarding this gorgeous view, but you should come to the top of the mountain with me."

Reyna shook her head, wondering where this sudden invitation was coming from. What did he want from her? "I don't do snow sports. I just like to play in snow."

"Then come play with me."

His gaze was searing, hotter than the water covering her flesh and even more tempting. Before she knew it, an agreement tumbled from her lips. Satisfaction flashed briefly in his eyes before he stood up and passed her the towel.

"Don't think this little playdate means I'm just going to fall into bed with you." Reyna shot him a look.

"I wouldn't dream of it," Garrison murmured.

She slipped from the water and quickly dried herself before pulling on her calf-length parka, socks and boots. She tried not to be self-conscious wearing next to nothing in front of him, but it didn't quite work. Garrison made her hyperaware of her femininity with the way his eyes devoured every inch of her bared flesh before she had donned the heavy coat.

But he didn't touch her or offer to dry her off as she imagined some men would have done. "Where should I meet you?" she asked.

"I'll come by your cabin," he said. At her skeptical look, he shook his head. "No games. You'll need more time to get ready, and I have to get a few things from my place first."

Despite what she thought about Garrison, it never occurred to Reyna that he would try something she didn't want. She only worried that she would be the one throwing herself at *him*.

"Okay," she agreed. "Meet me in half an hour. I'm in cabin number nineteen."

"Good. I'll see you there."

They parted ways on the private walkway toward the more isolated cabins. He continued even farther back, and she watched in surprise as he unlocked the cabin where she and her friends usually stayed. Reyna fumbled her key in the lock, paying more attention to a sudden thought—did he now sleep in one of the beds she'd slept in before?—than getting into her own cabin. She finally opened the door on the third try. By then, Garrison had long disappeared through his door and shut it behind him.

Idiot.

But once the thought of him in her bed came, others like it naturally followed.

She easily imagined him sprawled in the bed where she once slept. Spread out on his back in pajama bottoms—bare-chested, of course—and reading through briefs or whatever it was that workaholic lawyers did on vacation.

Or did he sleep naked? Reyna stumbled on the perfectly smooth living room floor of her cabin, cheeks burning, even though no one else could see.

Stop your foolishness, she chided herself.

In her room, she didn't waste any time. She quickly showered, smoothed lotion into her skin and dressed in her thickest snow gear. She was sitting on the couch and pulling on her boots when Garrison knocked. He stood in the doorway wearing the same outfit she had just seen him in, except he had goggles perched on his head instead of sunglasses. His gaze skimmed with appreciation over her body.

She welcomed him in. Thankfully, she and her friends had kept it relatively neat. Only a few items scattered here and there, including the nearly empty liter bottle of Baileys Irish Cream on the kitchen counter, hinted at what they'd been up to since being in the cabin. When Garrison glanced toward the bedrooms, Reyna ignored the speculation in his eyes.

She grabbed her yellow parka. "Let's go."

He took her to the aerial ski lift. It carried them high into the air, an altitude Reyna was used to from making the journey with her friends. But there was something different about being in the glassed-in car with Garrison. Anticipation curled in her stomach. As if she was about to do something both forbidden and dangerous. Jump off a cliff into the ocean. Take a rocket ship to Venus.

Reyna smiled at her fanciful thoughts. They sailed above a dizzying drop, high above bright white snow, majestic trees and a few intrepid souls hiking the route. The car, though large enough to hold at least ten people, was nearly empty and swayed with the wind.

"So where are we going?" she asked. "Should I be worried?"

A few seconds of silence ticked by. "The days of me hurting you are in the past," he said.

She looked away from his intent stare and fiddled with the cuff of her glove. They got off the lift far from the highest peak, where she suspected her friends were. Instead, they made their way through a noisy area with the sound of laughing children, the wind through the trees and excited conversation from more people than Reyna could see. They walked under a sign that said The Tube of Your Life.

They were going *tubing*.

"Are you serious?" She stared at Garrison.

"You said you wanted to play, so let's play." He tipped an eyebrow at her. In Garrison-speak, she was beginning to realize, this amounted to a smile.

The tubing area was a wide stretch of downhill slope, snow-covered and smooth. Very steep. Eight divided troughs of snow stretched all the way down the hill. The snowbanks between each trough were no more than three feet high. Rubber mats that slowed down the speed of the tubes rested at different intervals near the end of the downhill trail.

In brightly colored tubes, both children and adults hurtled down the slope at wild speeds, most of the women and children screaming, the men shouting out their macho calls.

Garrison paid for their tickets and grabbed a bright blue tube for each of them, and they were off.

"Are you sure about this?" she asked as she stared down the hill in consternation.

"Absolutely."

He smiled, an unexpected flash of white teeth against his clay-colored skin, and held the rubber tube for her to step into. She drew a quick breath, stunned by the beauty of that smile, realizing this was the first time she was seeing it. Reyna smiled back at him.

She automatically curled her gloved fingers in the straps on the top of the tube, convinced that otherwise she would fall out and break her neck. Garrison climbed into his tube then held on to one of her straps.

"Ready?"

"Not really."

"Perfect."

With his tube in front, he propelled them down the slope. They hurtled down the hill at God knew how many miles per hour while Reyna screamed with the surprise of it all. Snow flew up into her face, cooling her cheeks even more and getting her wet. She screamed while he laughed, and their tubes bumped together. They spun beneath the wildness of the blue sky as more snow flew into her face. Garrison's deep and booming laughter rained over her like confetti.

Her tube bumped against the snow wall then stuttered over the rubber stops. Reyna was breathless from her screams and laughter when they hit the bottom of the slope. She struggled out of the tube and to her feet with Garrison's help.

"Again?" she asked.

"As many times as you want."

They spent the rest of the morning and afternoon on the mountain, going up and down the slope until Reyna was too exhausted to do it anymore. She was surprised with how accommodating and gentlemanly Garrison was, making sure she was doing all right, checking with both his words and his eyes. Reyna had to keep reminding herself of who he was, what he was and what he had done. The blazing sun of their unexpected snow day threatened to melt all that away.

"I think I'm done!" She gasped, laughing, when her tube triumphantly bumped to a stop for what had to be the twenty-fifth time at the bottom of the hill. She wasn't the only one who was done. Around her, a few children were laughingly sprawled out in their tubes while their parents dragged them, tube and all, across the snow.

Reyna's face tingled from the cold, and her teeth felt frozen. The muscles from her arms ached from dragging her tube over the snow—she'd insisted, although Garrison offered to carry it for her. But the happiness bubbling inside her, unexpected and pure, made it all worth it.

Reyna tumbled against Garrison, and he caught her easily, letting go of the strap of his tube. Their gasping breaths frosted the air. Reyna braced her hands on his chest. "That was *so* much fun." She dropped her head back and grinned at the sky. The hoodie of her parka fell off her head.

Garrison pulled it back up with his usual restrained smile. "Good. It's no less than what I wanted for you today. The view from your hot tub is beautiful, but

I'd much rather have you here like this." His arms slipped around her waist. "I love the way you laugh."

The smile faded from Reyna's face at the serious look in his eyes. "Garrison, I don't..." Her voice trailed off into nothing. This was the time for her to tell him to stop touching her, to stop looking at her as if their lovemaking was a forgone conclusion. But the words died in her throat.

He smelled like fresh air and sweat, pine trees and a hint of the aftershave he had used that morning. A bolt of awareness darted inside Reyna. Up close, his long-lashed eyes were full of emotion, but none that she could name. How could she have thought this man cold and unfeeling?

Everything around them faded. For Reyna, it was just the two of them and the growing warmth in her belly. She felt an overwhelming need to kiss him.

His actions completed her thought, cool lips touching hers gently. She sighed and draped her arms around his neck, deepening the kiss. *Ah.* Want snapped between them, the instant spark of desire that picked up where they'd left off the night before. *No.* Her mind protested, called her a traitor. But her body melted shamelessly for him.

It was as if they still stood under that snow-laden sky, the evening cold and hard while the passion between them was a hot and honeyed thickness that threatened to drown her.

His tongue was firm and hot in her mouth, his hands solid on her back. Through the layers of clothes, her body flushed and readied itself to receive him, growing damp and swollen. Reyna whimpered and pressed closer.

What she had meant to be a shared kiss of celebration, an acknowledgment of the childlike pleasure they shared tumbling down the hill, suddenly became something else. Knee-weakening. Overwhelming. She ached to feel his hands on her. Inside her.

"I bet they're on their honeymoon."

The too-close voice dragged Reyna abruptly from her fever. She pulled away at the same time Garrison did. His eyes had darkened to nearly black with his desire. He cleared his throat and licked his lips. Reyna fought the urge to do that for him, stroke her tongue along the full curve of his mouth, sink her teeth into the beautiful flesh.

What's wrong with me?

Garrison cleared his throat again, lashes falling down to hide his eyes. When he looked at her again, his expression was calm. He said her name and touched a gloved finger to her cheek. "Let's go get some hot chocolate."

She pressed her damp and swollen lips together. "Okay," she breathed.

They left the slopes for the lodge and a table by the fireplace, the same one Reyna and her friends had watched him occupy the day before. She felt pleasantly worn, her muscles stretched and invigorated, especially her smiling muscles. It had been a long time since she'd had that much fun with a man. It had been even longer since she just relaxed and let someone else take control of her day. It felt good. For now, she would ignore what had flared between them at the very end, the nearly overwhelming desire to drag him back to her bed and feast on him until they were both satisfied.

While Garrison got their drinks, she sat at the table with her mind in turmoil. He was attractive. But he was also *the* Garrison Richards. Ruthless lawyer. Workaholic. Out of her league. It didn't seem smart to get involved with him, in any capacity. But it was difficult to forget the way he had handled her sketches and how perfect his lips felt against hers. Reyna's insides had already melted for him just a little.

"I hope you don't mind all this whipped cream. The guys in the kitchen must think you deserve something extra special." Garrison put a large mug of hot chocolate in front of her. Or she assumed there was some hot chocolate beneath the gorgeous hillock of whipped cream, chocolate chips and trails of fudge. His eyes danced.

"Oh, my God!" She laughed, nervous about picking up the mug. It looked as if one small breath would tumble the whipped cream all over the table, or over her. "I didn't even know it was possible to make them this big. I'm scared to drink it."

Garrison sat down with his own cup. "Don't be nervous. It's all about technique." He pulled the cup between them. "Come, let me show you." He invited her with a twitch of his fingers to mimic his movements.

Reyna giggled. "Really?"

"Don't be a coward."

He bent his mouth to the dark-and-cream concoction and sucked. His mouth came back with a smear of whipped cream. He effectively licked it away. "Now your turn."

She bit her lip, smiling. She was nervous that following his technique might result in inhaling a chocolate chip. Reyna tipped her mouth toward the cup and licked. "Mmm. That's good."

Across from her, Garrison's face grew hard. His eyes fastened on her lips. Suddenly self-conscious, she licked her mouth and tasted the remnants of whipped cream and fudge. "You're right, this is much better." She licked the hill of cream and chocolate chips, sighing in pleasure at the combined flavors on her tongue.

"I'd respectfully ask you to stop doing that." His voice was a deep growl. For the first time, she noticed the signs of his arousal, the darkened eyes, the way he couldn't stop staring at her mouth.

"Oh!" She turned away from his lust-darkened eyes. "Sorry."

Garrison shifted in his seat. "Are you, really? You know I'd gladly watch you do that all day, especially if we could take the cup back to my cabin."

He had to be joking. She quickly shook her head. "I don't think that would be very smart of me," she finally said once she could speak. But the traitorous part of her wanted to see what would happen back in his cabin, with or without the aid of whipped cream and chocolate.

"I'm not thinking with my brain at this moment," he said huskily. "And, although I understand, I'm a bit disappointed that you are." A pained expression crossed his face. "And I'm only kidding a little." He cleared his throat and shifted again in his chair. "Do you want some lunch a little later?"

Yes. Lunch. *If it involves spreading you out on a blanket and having my way with you.* She bit the inside of her cheek at the thought.

No. No. No.

But her body wasn't listening to common sense. Lunch and a cathartic roll between the sheets with Garrison sounded better the more she thought about it. What could it hurt? Chances were that she'd never see him again anyway. "I'd love to—"

"Reyna!"

She turned when she heard her name. Bridget hurried across the lodge toward her. Her friend looked fresh and healthy from her morning in the snow and sun, but her face was twisted with worry. When Bridget got to her table, she realized her friend was on the verge of tears.

Fear tightened Reyna's throat. "What's wrong?" She jumped to her feet.

"It's Marceline." Bridget sobbed. "I don't know where she is. None of us do."

Chapter 6

Reyna gasped and gripped Bridget's cold fingers.
"How long has she been missing?"

"Since maybe eleven. We all went up on the hill
together, but then we just lost track of her. We've
called her cell, but there's no answer." She drew a
shuddering breath. "Please tell me you've seen her."

"No, I haven't. I just got down from the mountain
a few minutes ago."

"Marceline seemed okay, but I think it was all an
act. On the slopes this morning, she couldn't stop
talking about that assh—" Bridget broke off and bit
her lip. "Anyway, she seemed too distracted and sad
to ski. She said she felt lonely, especially since it's
Valentine's Day." Bridget grasped Reyna's fingers
until they hurt. "She fell behind, even though we tried
to keep an eye on her, and then she disappeared." Her

eyes filled with tears. "If anything happens to her, I'll never forgive myself."

Reyna agreed with Bridget's words. Although Marceline had tried to pretend for them, she hadn't been exactly stable since she announced that she was getting divorced. She never told them the reasons for her separation, but her friends had trusted she was doing the right thing.

Even with that, Reyna never thought of her as the suicidal type. But then again, she had never thought her friend would get a man's name tattooed on her body, either.

"Where is Louisa?" she asked.

"She went back up to the mountain to search in case we just missed her."

"Okay." Reyna bit her lip, a half dozen possibilities of Marceline's whereabouts flitting through her mind. She turned to Garrison. "I have to go."

"I know." He stood and picked up his gloves from the table. "If you'll accept my help, I can join the search."

"Okay." She turned back to Bridget. "Did you tell the staff here?"

Her friend nodded. "At first I wasn't sure if I should, since I didn't want her to be embarrassed in case it was nothing. But I finally told someone at the front desk, and they notified security."

"It's going to be okay," Reyna said, trying to believe her own words. "Go talk with security and get Louisa. I'll check the places I think she might be." She named all the places that Marceline loved at Halcyon.

"I'll probably go back up to the slopes with the

security guys to find her," Bridget said. "Whatever they think is best."

"Okay, okay." Reyna grabbed her gloves then zipped up her jacket.

She and Garrison quickly left the lodge. Reyna shoved her trembling hands into the pockets of her jacket and hoped that Marceline was all right. Even though Reyna had been with Ian since she was fifteen and married to him for nine years, it would have never crossed her mind to harm herself after their split.

"Divorce affects different people in different ways." Garrison's words were low and soft, as if he'd peeked into her mind. "She's going through her own process. I'm sure she'll be fine with support from her friends."

"I never thought it would be this bad for her. She has always been the most stable and well-adjusted of us."

They rushed out into the cold and down the walkway to the cabin Reyna shared with her friends. She opened the front door with hands that shook, hoping as the door swung back that her friend was sitting on the couch with a cup of hot chocolate and a romance novel to help her through her crisis. But the couch was empty. So was the rest of the cabin.

Reyna slammed Louisa and Marceline's bedroom door shut. "Dammit!"

She could feel Garrison throwing her concerned looks from by the door. He glanced around the cabin but said nothing, giving her some time with her turbulent emotions. The resort was a safe place to be. But if someone was determined to hurt themselves, there were almost endless options of ways to do it. A shiver of alarm pimpled her skin.

"What about your divorce?" Garrison's voice cut through her morbid thoughts.

He stood on the other side of the large living room, an odd presence in her very female cabin, standing among the casual wreckage of the women's belongings. Bridget's pink robe flung across the back of the couch, two coffee cups on the kitchen table next to a bottle of Baileys, Louisa's boots dropped haphazardly by the darkened fireplace.

Reyna checked the log of calls on her phone. Marceline hadn't reached out to her.

"What about my divorce?" She repeated the question, only half paying attention to their conversation.

"Because of your cheating husband, your life as you knew it for nine years was suddenly over. Didn't you have a hard time?"

This was the first time they had explicitly talked about her long-ago marriage, her feelings, other than anger at Garrison's role in its dissolution. She didn't like talking about it at all. Especially not with Garrison.

"It was hard, yes. But what happened to me then is nothing like what's going on with Marceline. Ian didn't drive me running off into danger without any concern for myself. He hurt me, but I never once thought of hurting myself because of him."

Garrison made a noise, as if he was pleased by what she said. Reyna looked at him with suspicion. But his face was as calm as ever. She realized then that her panic over Marceline had lessened somewhat. She was able to think more clearly. Reyna cast another narrow-eyed glance at Garrison, knowing then that distracting her had been his intention all along.

"We should leave," she said. "I don't know where she is, but she's obviously not here."

She checked her phone again, making sure it was on both vibrate and the highest possible volume. Fighting another flare of worry, she called Marceline, only to hear her friend's phone ringing in the next room. Evening was coming, bringing with it the colder temperatures and cutting wind that Marceline hated.

Garrison waited for her at the door. They stepped into the cold together. While they'd been inside the cabin, it had started snowing again, light flurries that swirled in the air.

He grunted and pulled his gloves higher above his wrists then adjusted his already tight scarf. Reyna allowed herself a small smile of amusement. He obviously *hated* the cold.

"Why would she even be out in this weather?"

"Emotional turmoil makes people do desperate things, especially when they're in the middle of a contentious divorce."

"You would know," Reyna murmured.

"As would you."

She bit the inside of her cheek. The snow was coming down even harder as they stood on the front steps of the cabin, considering which direction to go. It was Garrison's hand on her elbow that compelled her to move, urging her toward a path flanked by high trees that had a set of larger cabins beyond it.

"I just can't believe it." Reyna said the words through trembling lips. "Marceline has always been one of the strongest women I know." When she'd met and fallen hard for Daniel Keller, a handsome football player for the New York Giants, Reyna thought that would add joy to her life, not ruin it. "It must be the divorce. It must be."

"She could have been so in love with him, she didn't know what to do with herself once the relationship was over. Love can be a poison." Garrison spoke like someone who'd never had intimate and real experience with love, someone who only saw it as an abstract and awful notion.

Although Reyna half believed what he said, she wasn't ready to hear it.

"Have you been poisoned like that? Because unless you have, you really don't know." She hastened her footsteps through the snow-thick forest, deliberately breathing in the icy air to calm herself. "You can't understand."

"I've never been poisoned by that ridiculous emotion, thank God." He looked truly relieved. "But I have empathy. I didn't have to be in an abusive relationship to understand its impact on the victim."

She scoffed. "How? From television?"

"My mother, for one." His expression seemed deliberately mild. "Also some of my pro bono clients who are now homeless, thanks to the so-called love they once had."

Garrison didn't give Reyna the chance to feel sorry for him, or even be impressed that someone of his obvious status gave his services away free without batting an eyelash.

"We should check the back of the resort by the fence." He pointed to a snowy path leading deeper into the woods. Only a few footprints marred the trail. It was the same path she had walked just last night, where Garrison had kissed her.

Reyna opened her mouth to agree with him when she remembered something. The honeymoon cabins. Not long after their marriage, Marceline and her ex had come up to the resort. Her friend had gushed about her honeymoon cabin experience, the happiness in her face almost too bright for Reyna to bear.

"The honeymoon cabins!" Reyna grabbed Garrison's jacket. "I think she's there."

Those cabins were at the back of the property, often reserved by couples who valued their privacy. Most of them didn't even bother coming outside once at Halcyon, simply taking advantage of the breathtaking views, romantic surroundings and peace and quiet to make love all weekend. The next time she had seen Marceline, her friend was glowing and talked nonstop about the new meaning Halcyon had for her.

Reyna texted her friends to let them know where she was going, then she took off at a run with Garrison by her side. Night crept ever closer, the biting winds turning Reyna's cheeks to ice.

Garrison ran slightly ahead of her as they made their way toward the opulent honeymoon cabins that Reyna had only seen in catalogs and online. They were so far from the rest of the cabins that it seemed to take forever to get there, pushing through the freezing winds and calf-high snow.

Despite their reason for being there, the path to the honeymoon cabins seemed enchanted. The snowfall was lighter there, the path protected by high pine trees that swayed hypnotically in the wind and flooded the air with their crisp scent. White blanketed the land-scape. The outline of the half dozen isolated cabins appeared through the snow. Lights burned through windows. The smoke from chimneys trailed into the sky.

Through the wind, Reyna heard the sound of sadness.

She turned to Garrison, breathless from their run. "Do you hear that?"

They hurried toward the noise. Before she saw Marceline, Reyna knew what she would find. Her stomach twisted with relief and pity at the sight of her friend huddled on the front steps of the farthest honeymoon cabin. She was dressed for the snow in boots, thick pants and a hooded jacket. But it looked as if she had been sitting in the same place for a long time. She shivered with cold.

Marceline hugged herself and rocked from the force of her tears. The sound of her sobs racked the air. When she and Garrison saw her, he stepped back and Reyna rushed toward her friend and hugged her.

"We've been looking everywhere for you!"

As soon as they touched, Marceline gripped Reyna around her waist as if she would never let go.

"It's Valentine's Day!" she sobbed. Her face was cold and wet against Reyna's. "I don't have anybody." She trembled in Reyna's arms, teeth chattering in a way that made Reyna hug her tighter. "He brought me here for our first Valentine's Day together and told me he'd give me the world. But instead he took everything away from me!"

"You'll get through this, Marceline. You will." She pulled Marceline to her feet. "Let's go, honey. It's getting too cold for you to stay out here." Her friend shuddered and stumbled against her.

Reyna met Garrison's eyes over Marceline's head. "She's freezing!"

Before she could protest, he unzipped his thick jacket and gave it to Reyna. "Put this on her."

Once the jacket was firmly zipped over Marceline's small frame, he easily lifted her. "Let's get her back to your cabin."

While he walked quickly ahead of her, Reyna called her friends and let them know Marceline had been found. The door to the cabin flew back into the wall as Garrison strode inside with Marceline in his arms.

"She needs a hot bath and her friends." He rested her gently on the couch then retrieved his jacket. "I'll leave you alone. I think my presence is the last thing she needs right now."

He paused as if he wanted to say something else, but he only pulled on his jacket, nodded at Reyna and left. By the time she drew a bath for Marceline and coaxed her into the water, Louisa and Bridget were bursting through the cabin door. She heard their noisy entrance as she sat on the floor next to the tub, the water steaming around Marceline's form curled in the water. Marceline's cheek rested on her upraised knees, and she rocked back and forth in the water, crying.

Bridget ran into the bathroom. "Oh, my God! Is she all right?"

"I don't think so," Reyna said.

Louisa came in at a more sedate pace. She sat on the toilet seat and smoothed a hand over Marceline's hair. "Honey, you just can't do something like this without telling us."

"We'd actually rather you not do it at all," Bridget muttered. She sat down on the floor next to Reyna.

Marceline raised her head. "I'm sorry." Her voice shook. "I didn't mean to—"

"Shh, honey. It's okay." Reyna narrowed her gaze at Bridget. "Take all the time you need." With the small bowl on the edge of the tub, she poured hot water over Marceline's shivering frame.

They used to joke that, maybe other than Louisa, Marceline was the toughest of the four women. In college, she'd had a boyfriend she caught cheating and simply threw bleach on the clothes he'd left in her dorm room, then refused to deal with him anymore despite his pleas for forgiveness. Then she was out dating another boy within a month, equally carefree and fierce as if the first betrayal had never happened.

Marceline had always bounced back from anything the world threw at her. She talked things out with her three best friends, processed all the hurt then got over it. But not this time.

This shivering and helpless version of Marceline scared Reyna. If she, the strongest of them, could be brought so low by a relationship, then what chance did the rest of them stand? She saw the same worry in Bridget's and Louisa's faces.

"Don't worry, honey," Reyna murmured. "We'll take care of you. You don't have to be strong tonight. We'll be your strength." She poured more hot water over Marceline's back.

Bridget gathered a robe for Marceline while Louisa

left the bathroom. Reyna soon heard the sounds of the kettle in the kitchen, the dim flare of the gas stove.

"Let's get you in bed," Bridget said, holding up the robe.

They dried off an unprotesting Marceline and guided her from the tub and under the covers. Louisa brought hot tea spiked with rum for all of them and sat on the edge of the bed.

The women stayed with Marceline deep into the night, speaking softly of trivial things while the specter of her breakdown and grief surrounded them all. Although she knew what she was afraid of, and knew that Louisa and Bridget were scared of the same thing, Reyna didn't know how to say it. Or even if she should. The selfishness of her thoughts, however, kept her mouth shut.

The three women sat around their friend as if they were at a wake, keeping vigil over her sunken spirits. They drank their tea and stroked Marceline's back, distracted each other with nonsense until they all eventually fell asleep.

Reyna jerked awake sometime later, an abrupt motion that slammed her head into the headboard. She groaned silently, her mouth tasting of stale tea and sadness. She had fallen asleep on the bed with the other women. The queen-size bed was barely big enough for their twisted bodies—Marceline spread out under the covers, Bridget in a fetal position at the bottom of the bed, Louisa next to Marceline with her arms around her waist.

Only Reyna was still wearing her day clothes, the two layers of thermal shirts, pants and thick socks.

It was late. Nearly midnight, according to the clock peeking from behind Louisa's shoulder.

Reyna crept from the bed and to her own room. There, in the privacy of her empty bedroom, she sat in the dark and allowed the sadness to engulf her. Seeing Marceline like that brought painful memories of her own divorce rushing back. As she'd told Garrison earlier that day, she hadn't been destroyed by the divorce, but it had deeply shaken her foundations.

She wondered now, though, how close she had been to losing herself.

Over the past few months, she had watched Marceline shrivel in confidence, question her life and shut herself off from the rest of the world, as if that would somehow help deal with what happened with her husband. The shutting off was understandable. Reyna had done it herself. No man had gotten close to her in the years since her divorce. But to take withdrawal and pain as far as Marceline had? Reyna shuddered.

No. She would not be that. She would *not*.

Chapter 7

A knock on his cabin door pulled Garrison from a sound sleep.

He rolled over and squinted at his watch on the bedside table. Almost two in the morning. He blinked again at the time. Who the hell...? He threw aside the heavy blankets and rose from the bed, hissing when the relatively cool air washed over his bare chest and stomach.

"Who is it?"

The voice on the other side of the thick wood shocked him into quickly opening the door. A blast of cold chilled his skin, and he shivered, although he wasn't sure if the shiver was from the cold or because Reyna stood in his doorway at a very suggestive time of the night.

"Good morning," he said with a hint of irony. But his heart began a thick, heavy beat in his chest.

Her gaze flickered over his bare skin with surprise, lingering on his stomach, then on the pajamas hitched low on his waist before coming back to his face. "Can I come in?"

He pulled the door open wider. "Please."

Reyna looked tired. The corners of her mouth drooped with sadness, and her shoulders hung low. Dark semicircles smudged beneath her eyes. As she walked in, she scanned the cabin's main room, the fire he'd allowed to blaze while he slept, the files he'd left in a neat pile on the wooden coffee table. He'd kept the old-fashioned log cabin clean enough, just as efficiently tidy as his own apartment. But he'd made himself at home, setting up his iPod and mini speakers so he could play the music he liked without the restriction of earphones.

"It's hot in here," Reyna said. Her voice was soft, much lower than he had been used to hearing it.

"I like it hot."

"No kidding." She took off her jacket and gloves and pushed up the sleeves of her sweater. Her eyes dropped again to his bare chest before she turned away.

Her gaze on him was like a warm touch on a cold day. Distracting and infinitely welcome. He excused himself to get a sweater from the bedroom, quickly pulling it on before joining her again. "Can I get you something to drink?"

"So formal." She raised an eyebrow, though it was only a shadow of her normal attitude. "Maybe a glass of lemonade. It feels like a Georgia summer in here."

"I was going for more of a Florida winter." He grabbed a pitcher of iced cider from the kitchen. It was the same one they served at the resort. Once he'd tasted it that first day, he couldn't get enough. He'd asked the attendant to make him a batch to last him the entire weekend. As he poured a glass for Reyna, he thought it could very well be a metaphor for how he felt about the woman herself: one taste, and he wanted more.

When he returned to the living room, she'd already made herself comfortable. She added a fresh log and stoked the fire with a poker, her butt tilted up in the air. He paused to appreciate the view.

"You don't have to do that," he said. "I know it's a bit warm for you."

"Warm isn't necessarily a bad thing." She smiled briefly over her shoulder before continuing with the fire. "You know, this is the cabin we usually get every year. It's got the biggest master bedroom and best view of the sunrise."

He sat on the thick rug in front of the fire and put Reyna's cider on the hardwood floor near him. "My secretary booked it for me, probably months ago."

Garrison leaned back against the couch and admired the play of firelight over her serious face, the length of her throat, the curl of her fingers around the iron poker. Reyna was truly, truly beautiful. Since he saw her on the train, it had taken an act of will to control his reactions to her, both physical and emotional.

He'd faltered the few times when he kissed her—and she kissed him back—but here, in the isolation of his cabin, knowing that she had come to him, he released his control and simply enjoyed the madness that she evoked in him. His body hummed with his attraction for her. He imagined he could smell the faintly sweet lotion she'd used on her skin, the warm and feminine essence of her.

"You're a lucky man. This place holds a lot of great memories for me." She picked up her cider and sat next to him with her legs curled beneath her. "Thank you for this." She lifted her cup.

"My pleasure."

He waited for her to speak, simply enjoying the vision of her in his cabin, sitting quietly in front of the fire and watching the flames while taking occasional sips of her drink. "It tastes good cold," she finally said.

"Yes, it does." Garrison nodded in agreement. But he was sure she hadn't come over to his cabin in the middle of the night to talk about the flavor of his cider. He opened the conversational door. "How is Marceline?"

"She's asleep now." Reyna glanced briefly toward the door, as if she could see through it to where her friend lay. "But in the morning, who knows how she will feel?" She fell quiet again, her face pensive. "Why is it that women always seem to be the ones to lose the most in a divorce?"

"I think that's just a perception. Men lose, too. Most women just never see how much."

She made a noise of disbelief, a soft sound that made him want to pull her into his arms and comfort her. "I had been perfectly happy in my marriage. I thought my husband was, too. Nine years." Her fox eyes blinked slowly as she looked somewhere he could not see. "Ian and I dated in high school. We planned forever together. We were happy. Then

I found out he was cheating on me with some of the women he met at work."

At work. Garrison knew well enough what that meant. In the entertainment business, the lines between work and play were often blurred. He heard it enough from his movie- and TV-star clients. He saw it himself at their wrap parties and closed sets. Many costars ended up sleeping together. Some of those relationships ended in marriage, while others merely ended when it was time for the next project and the next costar.

"The cheating was terrible," Reyna continued. "But I thought we could move past it if Ian agreed never to do it again. But he didn't think he did anything wrong. He was beautiful, and the women on set were beautiful, too, he told me. Of course it was natural they would end up together. I couldn't deal with that. When I demanded fidelity, he demanded a divorce."

Her tortured gaze fastened on Garrison's face. "Why is it so damn hard for men to keep their pants zipped? No place in our vows did it say *I'll be faithful until somebody better-looking comes along.*" She drew a heavy sigh and shook her head. "I'm sorry. I don't know why I'm talking about this with you."

Garrison hoped it was because she was starting to trust him. Her story was a familiar one, but an ache grew in his chest at the thought of her being hurt. The urge rose in him to break every bone in Ian Barbieri's pretty face. "Is that what happened to Marceline? Her husband cheated on her?"

"She won't tell any of us what happened. That's part of why it's so hard for me. One minute she was strong, the next she was broken down into a million pieces." She gripped her cup between tense hands. "It's not a very fair world, is it?"

"It isn't. I agree." He chose his words very carefully, aware that she was still forming her new impression of him. "I take any promise I make seriously. But in my business, I meet a lot of men and women who don't."

Reyna relaxed her grip on the cup then put it at her side. "Truthfully, if it wasn't for my parents, who've been together since before I was born, I wouldn't think that it was possible to have a happily-ever-after ending." She gave a tiny shrug, a helpless gesture so at odds with her personality that it pressed an unexpected ache in Garrison's chest. "I think they look at me with disappointment and wonder why I never made it work with my ex."

"I doubt that."

"I don't." She smiled, although the expression did not reach her eyes. "Mama and Daddy think it should be easy for me to find a love as perfect as theirs, but not everybody gets to have that. Love doesn't find its way to everyone's home."

She sounded resigned and sad. Never mind that she only echoed what Garrison felt about love and relationships in general. But to hear Reyna say the words sounded wrong on a visceral level. And yet he didn't know how to take that particular ache from her heart.

Garrison opened his mouth to give her some platitude about love and forever, but couldn't make himself say anything so empty. Instead, he allowed his attentions to be distracted by a hint of a design on her lower arm, a curled tendril of dark green. A tattoo.

"What's that on your arm?" he asked.

Reyna looked almost grateful for the subject change. With a pained smile, she rolled her sleeve down, completely obscuring the beginnings of what Garrison had seen.

"Ivy leaves," she said.

"Can I see?"

Reluctantly, she bared her arm again. A black ivy leaf with tender vines dipped from the scrunched-up sleeve of her sweater. More of it disappeared above her inner elbow. It was like a layer of fine black lace on her caramel skin.

"It's beautiful," he said. "Can I see it all?"

She flashed him a more genuine smile. A thawing. "We don't know each other well enough for that yet."

He fought a full-on grin when he realized what she said. *Yet.* "The evening is still young. And I can keep my fire going all night long just for you."

"Do you ever stop?"

"Only if you want me to." This time he did smile. And he could feel her responding to him, pulling herself from whatever fever she had been suffering through since her friend went missing. He doubted that she even knew why she had come to his cabin. She seemed content to simply sit by the fire and sip her drink. Except she kept shoving at the sleeves of her sweater, obviously getting overheated.

"You can take that off if you like," he said. "I assume you're wearing something else underneath. I know it's warm in here."

"Thanks. I think I will take you up on that." Reyna tugged off her sweater, leaving her form clad in a pale blue long-sleeved shirt. She sighed and tossed the sweater behind her. "Why do you keep it so hot?"

"I like it hot." Garrison unabashedly stared at her newly revealed skin, the seductively angled clavicles, her slender arms. "I grew up in Tampa, where the weather is consistently warm most of the year. Even though I've been in New York since college, I never got used to the cold." He shrugged without apology. "I keep my apartment warm year-round."

"I'm sure that only encourages all the women you entertain to take off their clothes around you."

"All the women?" Is that what she thought he was about? "Why would you say that?"

She laughed, curling a finger around her necklace and moving the charm—a star?—back and forth across the chain. "Are you fishing for compliments, counselor?"

"Not at all." Garrison dipped his eyes below the slow and seductive motion of her finger at her throat. Her skin was luminous in the firelight. "I am simply curious what you think of me."

A touch of color moved under her cheeks. "I think you know very well what I see." She tilted up her chin, facing him head-on with her forest-dark eyes. "You're an attractive man. There's an undeniable masculinity about you that I imagine women find hard to resist."

"Do *you* find me hard to resist?" He raised an eyebrow, teasing. Assuming she wouldn't play the game.

"I do."

Her reply stunned him into silence. For the first time, he didn't have a ready answer. This was what he wanted, but he had not really expected to get it.

Garrison cleared his throat. "Is that why you're in my cabin at this time of night?"

She blushed again but did not back down. "You knew it was me at your door. Is that why you answered without a shirt?"

He smiled, warming to their game. "You know answering a question with a question won't lead me astray from my original point, don't you?"

"I've heard that you're relentless. In your work."

"In play, as well."

She shook her head, a spasm of a smile moving over her mouth. "I don't think I'm in your league."

"You're very wrong about that."

"So…" Reyna drawled out the beginning to an abrupt conversation change, making no attempt at subtlety. "What made you decide to become a lawyer?" Their game was over then.

He allowed her to retreat. "My mother," Garrison said. "She raised me on her own with very few resources. I wanted to thank her properly for all the sacrifices she made for me over the years. I wanted to be able to give her the things she never had. Short of becoming a crime boss, being a lawyer seemed one of the easier ways to provide for her and for myself."

Her eyes widened as he spoke. He could tell that he had surprised her.

"I would've never thought you came from a single-parent home."

He shrugged. "It's nice to know you thought of where I came from."

"Conversation with you never goes where I assume it will," Reyna said.

"That's good. I am a lawyer, but I like to think I still managed to escape being boring."

"You're never that." She smiled again. But he could sense the discomfort in her. A restlessness that had not been fully eased by their small talk. "I did think you were boring before, but not now."

"What about you, Ms. Allen?" He teased her with her last name. "What made you decide to become a tattoo artist?"

Her wry laughter filled the cabin. "Desperation."

"Really?" He didn't hide his surprise. "You don't strike me as the desperate type."

"After the divorce, that was the only job I could find. It was either take that position or risk being homeless." She gave him an arch look. "I've never tried being without a place to lay my head, but I hear it sucks."

"I don't think that lifestyle suits anyone."

"True enough." Reyna toyed with the handle of her mug, her slender fingers hypnotically stroking the white ceramic. "I've been working at the studio for about five years now." Garrison watched her fingers, their slow and seductive motion leading his thoughts astray. He wondered how they would feel against his skin, or tangled with his as he sank between her thighs and she sighed his name.

He forced his attention back to their conversation. "But you say it's a pit stop."

"Yes. I'm a graphic artist. I have a degree in it and everything." She seemed almost embarrassed to share that with him. Her head dipped, and her lashes fanned down to hide her eyes. "I've been tightening my résumé and getting ready to shop myself around to ad agencies in the city."

"The tattoo studio thing getting too old?"

"No, I'm getting too old for *it*. The boys there are kids. I'll be thirty-three in a few months. Way too old to be hanging around what feels more and more like a frat house."

"You're beautifully seasoned." He stroked her with his eyes. "Hardly too old, but certainly too talented to stay in a place you've outgrown."

The flirtatious words flowed easily from his lips, surprising him. But his body had always been light-years ahead of his mind, knowing what he wanted and reaching out to take it before his always overprocessing brain could finish its particular set of analyses.

"Talented?" She toyed with her necklace again. "You don't even know my work."

"I've seen your sketches. I know your talent," Garrison said. "But I'd love the chance to know *you*."

The light from the flames flickered over her skin, creating shadows on her face, pulling him closer to her seductive warmth. She licked her lips and watched him.

"Will you give me that chance?" He held out his hand.

At first, he thought she would refuse him, fight the impulse that had drawn her to his cabin in the first place. He could feel the longing in her. He understood what she needed. Her friend had fallen apart in the wake of her shattered heart; Reyna wanted to prove to herself that she was stronger than that, that she did not rely on a man's ring on her finger to hold her together.

He could already see that she was strong. She had

rebuilt herself from a shell-shocked new divorcée into a resilient Circe who commanded his attention and interest like no other woman before. She didn't need a man to hold her together, but she wanted a man, *this* man, to hold her.

When she took his hand, the breath left his lungs in a silent rush. Her fingers curled around his, as if he was a cool mug of apple cider, and she longed to taste. She was warmer up close, her clothes and skin crisp with the scent of pine. Reyna smelled as if she belonged out there in the wilderness with the snow and trees and all the untamed beauty beyond his doors. He felt privileged to hold her in his arms.

"I'm glad you came here tonight." He kissed her.

The sweetness of her lips nearly undid him. Reyna sighed into his mouth and pressed her beautiful length into him, her fingers scratching the back of his neck as their lips pressed hotly together.

"I didn't come here for this," she whispered. "I promise."

He nibbled her lower lip, slid a hand under her shirt. "Whatever the reason, I'm glad you're here."

Garrison kissed her deeply, her mouth soft under his, the passion building between them quickly, a steady fire that rolled heat beneath his skin, flared a wick of lust in his middle and made him gasp with the surprising power of it. The fire seemed to claim her just as swiftly until their mouths were fused together, their breaths meshed. His pulse felt as if it would jump out of his throat at any moment.

He'd had his share of lovers, but no woman had ever burned passion in him so completely, had ever made him want to drop to his knees and worship and kiss her every inch up and then down again.

"I want to make love to you." He murmured the words into her throat, his hands fisted in the thick bounty of her hair.

"I thought that's what you were already doing?"

Garrison smiled against her skin. Needing no further invitation, he peeled the clothes from her body, enjoying the slow unwrapping.

He hissed in soft surprise at the beauty he uncovered. The lace of ivy curled from her arm, around her biceps to her shoulder. Black ink on brown skin. A stunning work of art that covered one shoulder blade like the remaining wing of a fallen angel, the scattering leaves in a swirling pattern across her back and one hip.

Reyna sat, naked, on the plush white rug while the firelight played over her soft skin. Her fox eyes watched him, unblinking.

"You take my breath away," he said.

Color rose in her cheeks again. "It's okay. You don't have to say that. I'm already going to let you into my pants."

Amusement and desire warred in him. How could she make him want her so powerfully and also want to laugh at the same time?

"Now it's your turn." Reyna jerked her chin toward his still-clothed body.

Garrison quickly lifted, unzipped and tugged until he was as naked as she was. Her gaze touched him everywhere, from his shoulders, down to his chest, his stomach. Her eyes lingered at his hips, on the proof of his desire for her. She licked her lips, and her tongue flicked out to touch her upper lip. The sight of it sent a bolt of pure desire through him.

"Come here," she murmured.

He came.

Hard body. Hard intentions. The fire of his lust propelled him into her waiting arms. He wasn't sure what he'd done in his life to deserve the pleasure of her body, the gift of her desire, but he was grateful. Their tongues tangled again, her hands roving his back, his hips, inciting him. They only had a few hours of pleasure to share, but abruptly, he wanted more.

He wanted a whole weekend, even an entire month, of nights like this with Reyna. Those thoughts should have troubled him, but instead, they resonated with a sense of rightness. *Of course* he wanted her. She had been on the periphery of his life for nearly five years now, affecting his work. It only made sense that she was here, in the center of his personal life, sharing pleasure, and soon, sharing his bed. She touched the source of his desire, and he groaned into her hot throat. His thoughts scattered. His tenuous control broke.

In moments, she was beneath him on the rug before the fire, her back arching as he bit her throat and thumbed the firm peaks of her breasts. Her flesh was miraculously female, soft as silk and as necessary as air. Reyna gripped the back of his neck when he settled his mouth on her breast.

"Oh…"

He worshipped her body. Telling her with his mouth and hands how much he wanted her, how much he desired her, that the world beyond the door

of his cabin didn't matter. Not for many hours yet.
She writhed beneath him. Loveliness. Responsive.
Stroking his body, digging her nails into his back.

Her thighs fell open to receive him, and Garrison groaned. The scent of her sex was like perfume,
weaving in the air around him, pulling him deeper
into the magic of her. He stroked her welcoming flesh.
She was damp and plump, ready for him. She moaned
his name, arched her glistening breasts to the ceiling
while he caressed her wetly, and she sang her song of
desire and pleasure for him.

Her nails scratched his shoulders. Her sex clutched
fiercely at his fingers. Her face was all beauty, her
eyes tightly closed, her lips parted, her thighs flung
open to hungrily grasp at the pleasure he gave.

"Oh, God…"

Her breasts quivered with each sharp breath she
drew. Unable to bear the temptation any longer,
he tasted them again. She shuddered beneath him,
fingernails scoring his back. The pain of it barely
fazed him. He kept going, loving the feel of her
around his fingers, the sweet heat of her sex, the
scent of her passion, the firm buds of her nipples
sliding beneath his tongue. Then she cried out, quiv-
ering beneath him, a perfectly plucked bow.

He reluctantly pulled himself away from her shuddering body and grabbed his jeans, his wallet. Garrison sent a silent prayer of thanks that the condoms
were still there.

She sat up, panting softly, her body a flickering
mystery in the firelight. "Let me do that for you."

Reyna took the packet from his hand. Her eyes
captured his as she tore the foil with her teeth. Gar-

rison gasped when she touched him, her fingers a slow torture, a delicate dance of passion that made him want to instantly bury himself into her lush wetness. The breath shuddered from him as she finished sheathing him in the latex. Watching him carefully, she climbed into his lap and slowly, slowly lowered herself onto him.

He gasped, pleasure flooding into him with each millimeter clutch of her drugging heat. He held on to her. She held on to him. They moved together, a single animal, racing toward its pleasure. Her sex twisting on his lap, her gasping breaths. He gripped her hips and buried himself deeply, stroked the sweetness into her.

Reyna threw her head back and cried out as she came apart around him. The light kissed her long neck, her damp lips, the graceful heave of her breasts. Garrison gripped her hips harder, slamming up into her. The groaning pleasure exploded in his body, obliterating everything but the wet heat of her around him, the feel of her sweaty, slick body against his. His heart raced.

Reyna lifted her head, her eyes already drooping with fulfilled desire and exhaustion.

An unfamiliar tenderness welled up inside Garrison. He stood, keeping their bodies joined, and easily lifted her delicate weight. Her legs tightened around him, and she sighed.

He kissed her throat. "Let me take you to bed."

Reyna only murmured sleepily in reply.

from touching his hard chest, the abs that curved beneath his skin like silken steel. Her hand wandered lower, where his body was already anticipating her touch. He drew in a breath.

"Yes, it is a very good morning." His hands spanned her hips.

"I have morning breath," she said when he dipped his mouth toward hers.

"What does your breath have to do with this?" But he didn't kiss her.

Instead, he licked her collarbone, and she shivered. Her thoughts flew away with each touch of his mouth on her skin. His morning whiskers rasped against her throat, her breasts then her belly. Her thighs fell open beneath his wandering kisses.

"Oh!"

He treated her like breakfast, as if he hadn't had a meal in weeks. His mouth was tender on her furred flesh, then on the center of her desire, a sweet magic that left her gasping. Reyna clenched her hands in the sheets as he made love to her with his mouth, the sounds of pleasure escaping her, uncontrollable.

"I love how you taste," he murmured into her wetness. Then proceeded to show her just how much.

Her back arched with each movement of his tongue. She undulated on the bed, sunlight burning beneath her skin, her breath coming quickly while he made her moan his name over and over again. He hummed against her, stroked her completely inside and out. Soft, then hard, then soft, hard again until she came apart with a scream, her body electric with its release. Reyna was barely aware of him kissing her thighs and her belly, making his way up her body.

She heard the sound of foil crinkling, then his hardness was between her thighs. Inside her.

"Garri—"

Again, the desire rose quickly, dashing her against the shore. Garrison captured her mouth as he moved inside her, deeply, passionately. His size stretched her, brought her a stinging pleasure. She gasped and locked her legs around his waist.

Reyna's body flushed with heat, and she clung to him, dug her nails into the firm muscles of his back. He hissed and moved faster, his sex thick and sweet in the heat of her. They groaned together, panted. The blankets tumbled from the bed, then the pillows. The headboard pounded into the wall. Reyna clung to Garrison, her life raft in the rocking sea of their lust.

His body plunged into hers, the perfect rhythm, the perfect pace. Then she was trembling again, shot through with white-hot bliss that made her hoarsely call out his name. Garrison quickened between her thighs, clutched her hips tighter. He spilled into her with a deep groan.

Reyna clung to him in the aftermath of her satisfaction, reveling in the sweaty heat of him, wanting to drown in it instead of rolling away in search of the coolness she usually preferred. His hard flesh called to the softness of hers.

She slid her arms up and around his neck, lifting her mouth for a kiss.

"What about your morning breath?" he asked with amusement in his voice.

She gripped the back of his head and pulled him down to press his heated mouth against hers.

He moaned into her, his hips jerking once between her thighs where they were still intimately joined. Reyna throbbed around him. The morning spice of his breath, tasting of both sleep and her feminine desire, made her moan in appreciation.

She drew back to gaze at him, and a sigh left her mouth.

"There's so much fire inside you," she murmured.

With wonder, she touched his throat where the steady pulse thrummed, his jaw that moved beneath her hands as he swallowed thickly under her caresses. Her thumb fit perfectly in the dimple at his chin. Reyna smiled.

It was a revelation, having him this close, to see the layers of the public Garrison peeled away to show this heavy-eyed and sensual man who actually cared. Before, while they'd played in the snow, and later, when he helped her search for Marceline, that man had peeked out. But now... Reyna's hands skated over his chest, the solid ridges of his stomach.

Garrison made a low noise and stroked her back, her hips. He was tired of being looked at and wanted to taste, that much was obvious.

"Damn, you are absolutely delicious," he rumbled against her mouth. "I wish we had more than just this weekend."

Garrison slid a hand between them, and she gasped when he found the hard button of her pleasure, circled it, teased it with expert fingers. She whimpered with rising desire. But the weekend...the *weekend*.

Reyna wrenched her mouth from his with a gasp. Her friends! Marceline. The reason she was even here this weekend. She didn't want Marceline to wake up and realize she was gone and think Reyna wasn't there for her.

"I have to go!" She pressed her palms against his sweat-slick chest.

"I know." He kissed her, then slowly, achingly withdrew his still-firm flesh from hers. "Don't worry, it's early."

But with more than a little regret, Reyna slid from the bed on rubbery legs. She tried to get her bearings before hunting for her clothes. She found them by the fireplace, discarded like confetti from a particularly wonderful celebration.

"Slow down." Garrison appeared from the bedroom, wearing only pajama bottoms that hung from his narrow hips.

She stopped with her T-shirt halfway over her head, unable to prevent herself from staring at him. He came to her with a hand towel. Without him saying a word, she knew what he intended, and she blushed.

"Let me take care of you so you can have a more comfortable morning once you leave here."

Then he dropped to his knees. Her face flamed, but she parted her thighs for him anyway and allowed him to wipe away the traces of their passion with the warm, wet towel. She squirmed at the thoroughness of his care, and her body responded despite his almost clinical touch. But she did not pull away. There was an undeniable confidence to him, a rugged masculinity about Garrison that was oddly amplified with him on his knees for her.

"Thank you," she murmured tremulously when he was finished.

"Believe me, it was my pleasure." He rose to his feet. "Now get dressed and go to your friends. I hope to see you later."

Yes, please.

Although her body flushed with the desire to climb back into bed with him right then instead of waiting for whenever *later* was, she forced herself to reach for her underwear.

She quickly finished dressing and left. With each step away from Garrison, she pushed him from her mind, focusing instead on the situation she had left in her own cabin just a few hours before. The sun was up, but that didn't mean her friends would be. At least she hoped not. The cabin was quiet when she walked in, the shades drawn. The only light flowed in through the kitchen window that they never bothered to shade. She quietly shut the front door.

"Where were you last night?"

She nearly jumped out of her skin. Louisa sat at the kitchen table drinking a cup of coffee. She still wore her nightclothes, black silk pajamas that outlined her slender shape. There were faint bags under her eyes, as if she hadn't really slept.

"I stepped out for a little while." Reyna glanced toward the closed door of her own room, wishing for an escape from the coming interrogation. She wondered if anyone else was awake.

Louisa's eyes were pitiless with amusement. "They're all still sleeping. I came out here a few minutes ago to think." But from the look on her face, she was done thinking and was ready to talk.

Reyna mentally sighed, resigning herself to talking about whatever it was that Louisa obviously had on her mind. She just hoped it wasn't her sex life.

"Did you spend the night with that sexy lawyer?"

So much for that hope. Reyna poured coffee for herself and sat down. "Yes. Yes, I did."

"Did you have fun?" Louisa asked. "You seem a little conflicted."

After a moment's pause, Reyna opted for the truth. "I *am* conflicted." She traced the rim of her coffee mug, the deep swirl of dark, hot liquid reminding her of Garrison. His touch. The way he tasted. "It felt good to be with him, but…" *It shouldn't.*

"He's your ex's lawyer, I know." Louisa made a dismissive gesture at Reyna's look of surprise. "It only took a few minutes with Google to figure that out."

Reyna's face grew hot for the third time that morning over Garrison. She took a hasty sip of coffee to buy herself time to respond. Her thoughts were confused, brain warring with body in just about every way the man was concerned. He was gorgeous. He made love to her with a tender fierceness she'd never experienced before. With him last night, the past hadn't mattered. But in the full light of day…?

"There's more to him than the ruthless lawyer I met before, Louisa."

"You don't need an excuse to have great sex, honey." Louisa steadily regarded Reyna through the steam from her coffee cup, her face serious. "Get yours without apology. I just don't want you to be hurt over this."

Louisa, for all her sharp edges, was the one among the three friends whom Reyna was closest to. She was also the one who knew her best. Louisa knew more than anyone just how unsettled the dissolution of her marriage had left her.

It hadn't been simply about Ian's infidelity, but about the trust she had lost, the disappointment in herself at being unable to make her marriage— something that was supposed to last a lifetime— work. While Marceline and Bridget had offered her money and a place to stay while things settled, Louisa gave her sound advice and the discretion of a confessional.

"I won't allow myself to get hurt," Reyna finally said. "I know what I'm doing."

But Louisa wasn't buying it. Her friend pursed her lips in disbelief. "You haven't been this preoccupied by a man in years. You need to be really careful."

"I will." But Reyna looked away, thinking of all the ways she hadn't been careful the night before. Against her good judgment, she had opened up more than her body to Garrison. She took a hasty sip of her coffee. "How is Marceline doing?"

Louisa gave her a look, but let her change the subject anyway. "I'm assuming she's fine. She actually slept through the night." Louisa smiled briefly, as if aware she was talking about their friend as if she was a baby. "I only got up about half an hour ago."

"Maybe she was just too exhausted. Especially after running all over the resort in the snow."

"Yes," Louisa said. "It's good that she slept. Maybe having us there gave her the comfort she needed to feel safe."

"Or maybe sleep gave her the only comfort available to her. It doesn't help that we were all in shock at seeing her like that." Reyna finally voiced the concern that had led her running into Garrison's arms. "She'd always been so strong. It killed me that that could happen to any one of us."

Instead of her usual cynical comment, Louisa only glanced down into her coffee. "I know."

They sat in comfortable silence, drinking their coffee while the sun rose higher, pouring its brightness into the kitchen and illuminating the blond wood of the old-fashioned log cabin table and chairs. The sunlight was warm through Reyna's clothes and reminded her of waking up in Garrison's bed—the heat of him, the passion they shared before she had to pull herself back to reality.

"It's okay to have this thing with Garrison, Reyna."

Damn. She controlled her blush with an effort. *Am I that obvious?* But she made herself look confused at her friend's unexpected comment. "What?"

"Just don't let him hurt you the way Ian did. It's easy to pitch off that emotional cliff when someone you love completely screws you over." Pain flickered briefly in Louisa's eyes. "Sometimes complete despair is only one heartbreak away."

When they woke up, Bridget dragged Marceline into the kitchen with determined cheer.

"Let's go for a soak in the hot tub," Bridget said. "I didn't bring this fabulous body up here to keep it to myself."

Marceline, who sat in her chair with shadows under her haunted eyes, smiled unconvincingly. "That'll be nice," she said.

They left the cabin, wrapped up in their long coats and thick boots, walking down the path with their arms around each other's waists while Bridget told them a horrible but funny story about being snowed in with an inept lover.

"After his third try, I was ready to claw my way out of that damn apartment, blizzard or not!" She laughed.

At the tub, the scene was as empty as it had been when Reyna was there alone the previous day. The overnight snow had been swept clear, and the water bubbled blue and chlorinated under the bright morning sky.

The women sank into the water with identical sighs.

"This is nice." Marceline splashed Bridget with a timid smile.

Her face was more engaged than she had been at breakfast. The sadness was still there, but that hint of lunacy from last night was gone. She seemed more in control of herself. Reyna was encouraged, but Louisa must have seen something in Marceline that she missed.

"You don't have to pretend with us," Louisa said to Marceline. "We love you whether you're happy or crazy as a damn three-dollar bill."

"Louisa!" Reyna poked her.

But a reluctant smile touched Marceline's mouth, this one more authentic than the last. "It's okay. I know what she means and really appreciate it. I just don't want to bring down the party."

"You have feelings, so what?" Louisa shrugged. "If you want to be Eeyore this weekend, you're entitled. Just know that when you get back to New York, you better get yourself together." Louisa leaned back in the tub and flicked her foot in the water to splash Marceline in the face. "You can break apart, as long as you put yourself back together."

Marceline nodded, looking simultaneously chastised and relieved.

For the rest of the morning, the women soaked in the water and talked about nearly everything. Surprisingly, Louisa didn't tease Reyna about Garrison. She only talked briefly about a younger man she was seeing in the Bronx who had an affectionate pit bull that always liked to get in the way while she and her boy toy were getting close.

"Ew!" Bridget made a face and giggled. "That's why I'm never getting any kind of pet. Animals and kids totally cramp your style."

"Only if you plan on staying single and unattached forever," Marceline said. "Do you?"

Bridget was unapologetic. "Who knows? Right now my life is perfect. Until I see a reason to change it, and so far I damn sure haven't, I'll keep living just like this. I'm having fun."

"Well, okay, then." Louisa gave her a high five.

"Hey, isn't that the cute guy from yesterday?" Bridget craned her neck to look over Reyna's shoulder.

"Oh, yeah." Marceline wrinkled her forehead in confusion. "Wasn't he...there last night?"

Butterflies in Reyna's stomach went crazy when she spotted Garrison. He was at least fifty feet away, nearly hidden behind a row of shrubbery, and walking down the path from the first cabin that served as a business office. He had a companion with him, a petite woman with long hair swinging from a fashionable fuchsia ski cap. She was beautiful and looked up at him as if he'd just created heaven and earth.

"Yes, that's him," Reyna said, staring at the woman. "He was really great yesterday, during the… you know."

She kept her tone of voice dismissive and light, hoping that only Louisa noticed her discomfort.

"Sorry I cramped your style with my freak-out," Marceline said, her mouth turned down.

"Stop talking foolishness. You didn't cramp anything." If anything, Garrison was the one derailing whatever it was they had going on. Just who the hell was that woman?

"So did you get laid or what?" Bridget's eyes went wide with the anticipation of a story.

Louisa surprised Reyna again by coming to her rescue. She flicked her hand across the surface of the water at Bridget. "Why is everything always about sex with you, Bridget?"

Bridget squealed and jerked back. "Don't you dare get my hair wet!"

That made Louisa act up even more, making bigger and bigger splashes. Then Marceline joined in, splashing everyone indiscriminately. Reyna shrieked as their peaceful soak degenerated into a water fight, and she managed to forget all about Garrison. At least for a little while.

After she and her friends dragged themselves back to the cabin, they showered and made a run to the lodge for one last meal before they had to go back to the city. They ate together, the mood much better than it had been before, lightened by their water fight and the shared laughter that followed. After their late lunch, they went shopping in the boutiques down the hill from the resort. They stayed together, trying on clothes, teasing each other, playing around in a way they hadn't done in a long time.

Reyna was holding up a bikini, one that was shocking pink and barely covered any skin, in front of her torso, playfully swinging her hips at Bridget, when she saw a familiar face. Garrison. Reyna felt a jolt of gladness at the sight of him, then immediately remembered he had been talking intimately with another woman the last time she saw him. A woman who very well might be her replacement in his bed.

Garrison stood at the jewelry counter, gorgeous in his thick gray jacket over a dark sweater and jeans. Effortlessly, she recalled what he looked like under his clothes, his dark skin glistening as he moved between her spread thighs. Reyna swallowed past her dry throat and tried to turn away. But something made him glance up then, and their eyes met.

Garrison said something to the woman behind the counter as she handed him a small package. Only then did Reyna look away.

"You'll definitely get all the boys in the yard with that piece of nothing," Bridget said.

But Reyna's light mood was gone. She put the bikini on the rack. "I'll be back in a sec," she said. She wanted, no, *needed*, to speak with Garrison.

"Oh, okay." Bridget shrugged and eyed the little bikini Reyna had just relinquished. "I'll be over here. Maybe buying this bikini."

Reyna walked quickly toward where she had seen Garrison, winding her way through the boutique and its elegantly displayed racks of clothes. He appeared at her side before she was even halfway there.

He said her name. Reyna stopped walking, felt her body drift toward his in the middle of the store, her skin seeking a reconnection, a touch of that spark from the night before. When he took her arm, she shivered.

"Can we talk?"

Without waiting for her answer, he whisked her to the back of the store and into an empty dressing room. He closed the door and clicked the lock shut. Instead of touching her as she expected, Garrison took a step back and shoved his hands into his pockets. The dressing room was large, but not large enough to comfortably accommodate them both. Reyna backed away from him and sank down onto the bench.

"What's on your mind?" She gripped her purse in her lap to give herself something to hold on to. With him so close, she couldn't even remember what she wanted to talk to him about.

"You."

Her stomach fluttered, an annoying habit it was developing around him. Even under the harsh fluorescent lights, he was compelling, more attractive than any man had the right to be. He smelled like a long shower, and of a subtle cologne that made her want to lean closer.

"It didn't seem like you wanted to talk to me out there." Garrison leaned against the farthest wall, his body a beautiful incline that sharply reminded her of seeing him on the train that first day. Just then, the idea of him sleeping with someone else so soon after they'd been together was so ridiculous that she was ashamed of even thinking it. "Do you have any regrets about last night?" he asked.

No. Reyna took a breath, not quite wanting to tell him the truth. "I feel a little guilty for enjoying my night with you when Marceline was in such a bad way."

"There's nothing wrong with enjoying yourself and being happy," he said. "Even if it's for a moment."

For a moment. The words echoed in Reyna's head, an ominous and unwanted rumble.

Even though she had been the one to come into Garrison's room and initiate their lovemaking on purely temporary grounds, she realized a part of her—a stupid part—had wanted it to mean more. She wanted it to be something other than a *moment*. And the realization was a little embarrassing, especially since Garrison obviously thought of their night together as simply that, a *momentary* indulgence in pleasure.

She squirmed under the fluorescent lights, aware that they probably made her look twice as foolish as she felt. "I have to go back. My friends…" Her voice trailed off.

"I know." Garrison curled his fist around something in his pocket, and she felt his eyes on her face like a fleeting caress. He took a card from his wallet. "Make sure you keep it this time. Give me a call once you're back in the city."

His words sounded like such a blow off, if anything, an invitation to be a casual bed partner. And an invitation that he didn't seem to care whether or not she accepted. Embarrassment and chagrin burned her face as she took the card, careful not to touch his hand. She felt like an idiot for allowing her hormones to carry her along on this tide of attraction, ignoring what she knew about him in favor of what her body wanted.

"Okay." She put the card in her back pocket and stood up in the small space, the movement bringing her within kissing distance of him. Her hand fumbled for the lock on the door while her heart pounded heavily in her chest. "I'll see you."

He didn't try to stop her when she left.

A thick knot of disappointment sat in Garrison's throat as he watched Reyna walk away from him. He'd wanted her to stay and make concrete plans to meet again in New York. He was about to ask for just that when he saw the expression on her face. She looked uncomfortable with him in the small dressing room, as if she regretted everything they'd done together.

He gripped the small box in his pocket. He had meant to give it to her before they left the resort, as proof of something even he was not quite sure of. The night they shared in his cabin cracked open a door he'd thought firmly closed. Through that crack, he had seen possibilities, hints of a different life for himself. That night with her had meant more than just flesh meeting flesh, more than desires being sated under the cover of night. He wanted to let her know that.

That wish led him to thoughts of a gift. And because he hadn't known what sort of gift to give a woman like Reyna, he'd asked one of the staff at the resort. The woman had been friendly, a little too friendly, he realized later as she had walked with him toward the lodge.

Before Reyna, Garrison had never met a woman who affected him so strongly. He had essentially just started to get to know her, yet everything about her made him sit up and take notice. All his reservations about not wanting to end up like his clients—in love one moment and hating each other's every breath the next—let him know a long time ago that "happily-ever-after," or at least what passed for it in today's world, was not something he wanted to pursue.

But Reyna made him want to pursue *her.* She made him want. As he usually did after tense negotiations, he analyzed the strongest impressions of their last few minutes together in his head. The stiffness of her shoulders, the way she hadn't wanted to meet his eyes, and how she'd practically run out of the dressing room after reluctantly taking his business card.

What had changed between them since the morning in his bed? Earlier, she had been enticing and sexy, demanding as much pleasure as she gave, reveling in their lovemaking under the early-morning sun. But now, she was…different. He settled his hand again around the box in his pocket and left the dressing room.

In his cabin, he packed up his things in preparation for his drive to see a nearby client before heading to the train station.

His mother called. He answered his cell and dropped the overnight bag at his feet. "Hey."

"Are you actually relaxing this time?" she asked.

Garrison could hear the sound of a crowd in the background, conversations, a man's deep voice nearby.

"Of course." He smiled into the phone. "I love to relax."

"Garrison Felix Richards."

"Yes, Mother."

"Anthea told me how hard you've been working these past few months."

Just the past few months? Anthea mustn't be telling his mother everything. Garrison worked hard all the time. He knew it wasn't a healthy habit to cultivate, but how else was he supposed to get work done? He'd already set up healthy earning investments to pay for anything his mother wanted. She never had to work again. That was his goal when he started college. But after seeing to her comfort, working hard had simply become a way of life.

"I'm actually at a resort, Mother, if you can believe that."

"I do believe, but only because Anthea booked the tickets for you. I told her it was a good idea when she asked me whether or not to do it."

"I'm glad I don't have the misguided idea that I'm running my own life."

"Good!" She laughed. "Get back to whatever it is you were doing. I'm just calling to make sure you actually went to the resort. I wouldn't want Anthea to waste her time or your money."

"They're not wasted, Mother. I've enjoyed myself here. It's very invigorating being up in the mountains." He smiled, thinking of Reyna and her softness snuggled against him in bed. "I might even make this an annual thing."

"What? Don't make your poor mother have a heart attack." She actually sounded a little worried. "I don't know what brought on this attitude change, but I'm glad for it. You won't find a nice girl to settle down with if you're stuck in that office with the other sharks."

"Mother! This is your only son you're talking about."

"Exactly. I do like to think I know you a little. You're a shark for a good cause." A man's voice said something close to her. "Anyway, I have to go. I just wanted to check in on you. Take care of yourself up there, and don't get swept away in an avalanche."

Garrison chuckled. "I'll do my best."

"Love you, baby."

He heard the man's voice again. Whoever this person was, he was definitely with his mother. And he was a demanding guy, by the sound of it.

When Garrison hung up the phone, the smile fell from his face. He loved his mother, but she never made the best choices where men were concerned. As her son, he would defend her until the ends of the earth, but he knew her weakness was an idealized view of romance and men who promised her the moon and stars but only delivered heartache. That was where romantic entanglements often led. Nowhere.

He took the small box with Reyna's gift out of his pocket and dropped it on the bed. What had he been thinking? A gift for a woman who was all but a stranger? He grabbed his overnight bag and headed for the door. In the doorway of the bedroom, he paused and glanced over his shoulder at the box that

Chapter 9

In New York City, life went on as usual. Or at least, Reyna liked to think so. She went to work at the tattoo studio in Manhattan, took the train back and forth to her Brooklyn apartment, bought groceries and hung out with her friends when their schedules and needs permitted.

She did not think about Garrison Richards and what they had done together. She did not yearn for his touch in her lonely bed. She did not take out his business card, wishing that she was desperate enough to call him.

Days passed since the last time she saw him in that cramped dressing room. Then those days became a whole week. At the start of the second week, she ran his card through her shredder and took the papers to the recycling bin. As if she'd known exactly what Reyna had done, Louisa called to tease her about Garrison.

But she did not give in to the loneliness she felt.

Some nights she wished she had not opened that Pandora's box of need. After having a lover for the first time in many, many months, her craving—for Garrison, in particular—was a physical thing. Like the jitters she sometimes got from drinking too much coffee.

After a long afternoon and a late night at work, she opened her door at almost 5:00 a.m. to the ringing sound of the telephone in her apartment. Reyna frowned as she reached for it. Only her parents called her on her landline. She actually only had it because of them. Her mother was convinced that if Reyna needed 911, her cell phone would be of no use to her, and she would be dead in her apartment for days before the police came. Her mother watched the news too much. But Reyna kept a phone for her apartment and had an extra bill just because of her mother's paranoia.

Speaking of paranoia, she didn't recognize the number on the display. It was a Manhattan area code.

"Hello?"

"I was afraid you wouldn't answer."

She lost her breath.

"Don't hang up." Garrison's deep voice caressed her through the phone.

"I won't." Reyna's legs were shaking too much for her to stand up. She sank to the floor and sat cross-legged with the phone's base in her lap. "I'm surprised to hear from you."

"Well, you never called me, so I figured it was up to me to make the first move or risk missing out."

"What exactly would you be missing out on?"

"Your company." His voice dropped even lower. "The chance to wake up next to you again."

Reyna took a quiet breath, trying to ignore the memories his words conjured. That morning in the cabin. Sunlight. His mouth on her. The way he'd made her feel.

"This is real life," she said. "We're not on vacation anymore. You're not obligated to reach out to me."

"Who said anything about obligation? I want to see you."

"I—"

"Let me take you out to dinner." She heard the dim sound of papers rustling in the background. He was working. She wondered if he'd been awake for hours already, or like her, just had not gone to sleep.

"Why?"

"Because I want to." He paused. "Because *you* want to."

Her hand tightened around the phone, and she bit her lip. "You don't know what I want, Garrison."

"This, I do. I know what you want when my mouth is on your throat. I feel your pulse beating in your neck, your body's way of telling me how much you want me to—"

"Fine. I'll have dinner with you."

"Good." His deep voice resonated with satisfaction.

"But it's just dinner. I—" She wanted to say that she had made a mistake coming to his cabin that night, that they shouldn't have made love. But the words wouldn't come.

"I'm listening, Reyna."

"Nothing." She shook her head, although obviously he couldn't see her. "Pick me up on Saturday night at eight o'clock." Normally, she wouldn't have had the weekend free, especially since she just got back from three days in the mountains. But she had asked for time off to visit her parents. At the last minute, long-time friends of theirs had invited them to Mexico, leaving Reyna suddenly with a free weekend.

That sound of satisfaction came from him again. "I think I can handle that."

"Good. I'll see you then." Despite telling herself that it didn't matter whether or not she saw him, her heart thudded heavily, Saturday being only two short days away.

"Aren't you going to tell me where you live?" he asked.

"I'm sure you can find out that information the same way you found my phone number."

"You might have a point there." His laughter, rumbling and unexpected, teased her through the phone. "I'll see you then."

Reyna hung up and drew a trembling breath. What the hell had just happened?

She had been thinking intently of Garrison all day. So intently that she apparently conjured him up. She sat on her floor with the sounds of her neighborhood flooding through her third-story window: the rumbling of the subway nearby, reggae music pumping from a passing car, loud laughter and conversation in Spanish and an answering curse in Jamaican patois.

Her life in New York was so very far from Garrison Richards and the escape to Halcyon she had with her friends once a year. She wondered what he would think of her apartment when he saw it, what he would think of her life.

"It doesn't matter," she said out loud.

Annoyed with herself, she jumped to her feet and left the living room. But her words didn't stop the glad beating of her heart, or the humming song that left her throat as she showered in preparation for bed.

Later that morning, after waking much earlier than usual, she sat at her window seat, drinking her first cup of coffee. Snow was still on the ground, long ago turned to gray slush, but it was still beautiful. Far off, the buildings and streets of Brooklyn glowed with their winter magic. The cars bumped along the streets while the pedestrians wound past each other, heading to whatever was important to them at ten in the morning. Reyna loved it all.

Her phone rang, her landline again, pulling her from her window-seat musings.

"Is this Ms. Reyna Allen?"

"Yes, speaking." She automatically straightened her spine and hardened her voice at the sound of the professional tone coming through the phone. Was this about her parents? Her heart thumped wildly at the thought.

"Excellent. This is Amanda from the advertising agency of Kellerman-Stark."

Reyna frowned at the name of one of the biggest ad agencies in the city. "What can I do for you?"

The woman didn't seem at all fazed by her coolness. "I'm calling because Garrison Richards recommended you to us. Do you have time to come into the office this week and take a look around to see if we are the right fit for you?"

Reyna blinked. She never sent an application to Kellerman-Stark. It was one of the best in New York, maybe even in the United States. It had never occurred to her to reach that high for her first graphic design job. And the woman, Amanda, didn't sound as if she wanted to interview her; she seemed ready to offer Reyna her own office right then and there.

"Um. I'm sorry...Amanda. I really appreciate you calling, but I never applied for a job there."

"I'm well aware of that, Ms. Allen. However, based on what Mr. Richards said about you, we think you'd do wonderfully here."

Exactly what had Garrison said? That she was a good lay and frequently took initiative? Reyna's face heated with anger and embarrassment. "Okay. Thank you. Um...unfortunately, I won't be able to come in and check out your office. I'll wait until you've had a chance to at least look at my portfolio."

The silence on the other end of the line made Reyna check to see if they were still connected. They were. "Hello?"

"I'm sorry, Ms. Allen. It's just that you've surprised me."

"It's okay. I think I just surprised myself, too. Thank you for calling. I really appreciate you taking the time out of your day to get in touch with me."

"Very well. My apologies for wasting your time." There was wry amusement in the woman's voice.

"Have a great day. Maybe we'll be hearing from you later on and perhaps even see a portfolio?"

"Maybe. Thank you, Amanda."

"Thank you, Ms. Allen."

She very gently put the phone back in its cradle, even though her blood pressure soared through the roof. Who the hell did Garrison think he was? With this ridiculous job offer, he practically told Amanda and everyone at Kellerman-Stark that they were sleeping together. He was clearly saying she didn't have the talent to get the job herself.

Reyna grabbed the phone and quickly scrolled through her caller ID to get to Garrison's number. Her hand hovered over the redial button.

No.

She should wait and tell him in person what she thought of his patronizing and high-handed behavior. She ignored the gleeful voice in her head that said at least she would get the chance to see him before she wrote him out of her life for good.

Reyna left the phone alone. On Saturday she would see him again. Then she would tell him exactly where he could shove that job offer.

On Saturday night at eight o'clock precisely, her house phone rang.

"Good evening." Garrison's voice was a shivering pleasure through the line. "I'm downstairs."

Reyna, already dressed and ready for the past hour, peered in the small mirror near the door to double-check her lipstick. "Okay. I'll be right there." She hung up the phone and took a quick breath.

Her reflection said she looked fine. Her curls were

glossy and thick. They framed her carefully made-up face, the expression that said "look but don't touch." A safe, cream dress hugged her figure from throat to knee. She had been going for feminine and reserved. But the few pounds she'd gained since the last time she wore the dress made the presentation a bit sexier than she'd have liked. It was the most date-ready dress she owned, so she was determined to make the best of it. Black shoes and a black clutch completed the outfit.

Downstairs, she closed the door to her building and turned in time to see Garrison standing on the curb next to a dark luxury sedan. He was mouthwatering in a long black coat that fit just so over his wide shoulders. A houndstooth scarf neatly tucked into the throat of the coat lent him a faintly European air. After two weeks, seeing him again made her choke on her own breath. Had he gotten even sexier in that time?

As she walked toward him with her coat unbuttoned to enjoy the brush of the night's coolness on her skin, Reyna suppressed the desire to greet him with a kiss. To press her cheek to his and feel if he was as smooth shaven as he looked, or if his hidden beard would rasp against her skin, provoking goose bumps and impure thoughts. She tucked her purse under her arm and walked toward the car.

Garrison opened the door for her, his eyes appreciative on her figure and face. A touch of heat flared in his gaze.

"You look beautiful," he said.

"Thanks, so do you." She could have slapped herself for saying that. But she refused to stutter and correct herself. Men could look beautiful if they wanted to, dammit!

His eyes crinkled in amusement. "Thank you."

She slid into the passenger side of the black two-door Jaguar lush with the scent of leather and a subtly spiced aftershave. Garrison got in the driver's seat and put the car in gear. He glanced at her with another amused look.

"Thank you for coming out with me tonight."

"Don't thank me yet. You don't know how the night will end." She clasped her purse in her lap and glanced at him from the corner of her eye.

"That sounds ominous." He pulled the car into traffic with practiced ease.

Reyna said nothing. During the drive, she felt his curious gaze on her, but he did not interrupt the comfortable silence.

Minutes later, the car pulled into the only remaining parking spot in front of a small restaurant Reyna had never heard of, The Beautiful Feast.

The exterior was classic Brooklyn brick, with wide glass windows facing the street and only a dozen or so tables inside. The interior was elegant and sparse, the walls decorated with chic black-and-white photographs of celebrities from the early twentieth century. Dorothy Dandridge. Sydney Poitier. Eartha Kitt. Nina Simone.

A chandelier spun with hundreds of tiny crystals hung from the ceiling, scattering pieces of light into every corner of the restaurant. The hidden speakers played a haunting, old-fashioned song that Reyna didn't recognize. It was a beautiful place. Dimly lit and perfect for a date.

Reyna could easily imagine sliding her shoes off under the table and resting her feet on top of Garrison's while they shared their meal. But she quickly came back to reality and shook herself out of it. Dinner probably wasn't going to turn out that well.

A hostess, slim and gray-haired and with a welcoming smile, greeted them at the door. She seemed as if she could be anywhere from forty to sixty-five, a charming woman who exuded the same elegance and poise as the restaurant.

"Mr. Richards, it's good to see you again." She turned her smile and another warm greeting to Reyna.

"Your delicious food will always have me coming back, Ms. Taylor." Garrison took off Reyna's coat and then his and hung them on the coat rack near the door.

With the coat gone, Reyna saw that he was wearing a charcoal-gray three-piece suit, slim fitted, with a gray paisley tie. Could the man get any more delicious? She distracted herself from his body with a pointless rummage through her purse.

But the hostess was openly enjoying Garrison enough for both of them. "Please," she said with a brilliant smile. "I told you to call me Vivian!"

"Only if you call me Garrison." A genuine smile lit his eyes, and Reyna was almost jealous of the woman. But she kept her misguided poison to herself.

Vivian laughed and pulled two menus from behind the small hosting station by the door. "All right, Garrison. Follow me. We have your table ready for you, as requested."

She took them to a table in a far corner of the restaurant already set for two with wineglasses and tableware. A sprinkling of dark red rose petals lay on the white tablecloth, surrounding a trio of unlit votive candles.

Vivian took a lighter from her pocket and put a quick flame to the candles. "Enjoy your meal."

"Thank you."

Once Vivian left, Garrison pulled out Reyna's chair for her before claiming his own.

"This place is beautiful. Is this where you take all your women friends?" So much for not showing her jealousy.

The corner of Garrison's mouth lifted. He was laughing at her. "My mother has had dinner here with me. Also a friend or two. Otherwise, it's just my place to relax and get away from it all."

He did seem relaxed, despite the incredibly sexy suit that fit his body as if it was tailor-made, which it probably was. She could easily imagine him in an office, cloistered away from the rest of the world while he delved into the seedy underbelly of dissolved marriages, bitter separations and love gone wrong. Reyna took a deep breath to dismiss that thought from her mind. It wouldn't serve either of them very well.

A waitress came to their table. Small and quick, she was absolutely professional, treating them well but without the intimacy that Vivian had shown. She left them with glasses of water, Perrier for him and tap for her, and went to put in their order.

The restaurant was a fusion of African-American, West African and Caribbean cuisine. On the menu, fou fou and collard greens sat next to oxtails and stewed chicken. Fried chicken and waffles were served as a main course, with fried plantains as appetizers. The scent of Jollof rice and peanut soup wove like incense through the air.

"So." The wooden chair squeaked faintly as Garrison leaned forward, resting his forearms on the edge of the table. "What's on your mind so heavily today?"

The sleeve of his jacket slid down to reveal platinum cuff links. The letter *G*. Reyna's eyes dropped to his thick wrist, unable to look away from them and his long hands, the veins raised and prominent. What did a lawyer like him do to get hands like that? She swallowed and forced herself to look away.

She'd always had a thing for veins. And with him it wasn't just his veins. She remembered every inch of him revealed in the firelight that night as he'd touched her and brought her to the very heights of pleasure. Every inch of him was perfection.

She sat back in her own chair, deliberately keeping her eyes off his hands. She cleared her throat. "I don't need a sugar daddy."

He raised an eyebrow. "Where's that coming from?"

"I got a call from Kellerman-Stark on Thursday. They offered me a job, even though I hadn't applied." Faint traces of the anger she'd felt during that phone call snaked through her. "You can't buy me with a job, Garrison."

"That's far from what I was trying to do."

"Then what were you thinking? You don't know anything about my work. You've never seen my portfolio. For all you know, I can only draw stick figures and smiley faces." She tightened her jaw. "I resent you trying to manage my life like that, especially since we only spent one night together."

Across the table, his face grew tight. "What if I told you I want more than one night with you in my bed?"

She blushed, the thoughts exploding in her mind faster than she could control them. Him, naked in bed. Her, naked with him. His kisses. His slim hips pressing down into hers. "No."

"No?"

"Don't try to sidetrack me. I'm pissed that you're trying to handle my life. That's what I want to talk about, not how good things are between us in bed."

"Ah, so you *do* want to revisit what we shared in the mountains."

"I..." She pressed her lips together, censoring herself. "I enjoyed the time we spent together at Halcyon, but I was frankly surprised that you called."

He clasped his hands and watched her with the intensity of a hawk. "Wasn't the good time we had enough of a reason?"

"No. Good sex is as common as air—"

"Not in my experience," he muttered.

Not in hers, either, but she was trying to make a point. "Don't," she said. "Just don't." At his mock-innocent look, she drew a frustrated breath. "Don't dismiss what I'm trying to tell you like it doesn't matter."

"It does matter, Reyna. That's why I'm apologizing. I didn't mean to make it seem like I was willing to trade a job for more amazing sex with you. I'll take away all the jobs in the world if you'd just come home with me again." His mouth tilted up, but his eyes were completely serious.

Something fluttered in her belly, but she didn't relent. "It doesn't work like that."

"Reyna." Her name rolled off his tongue like a soul-deep caress. She shivered in reaction and clenched her back teeth against the pleasure of it. Garrison unclasped his hands to tap a forefinger very lightly on the table. "I enjoy your company. Very much. Please forgive me if I've seemed dismissive or like I wanted to buy you. It's not either of those things."

His tap against the table brought her eyes back to his hands. Reyna swallowed and forced her gaze back to his. Another bad idea. His gaze was a warm trap, the long-lashed brown eyes watching her with interest, admiration and more than a little desire.

"If this will convince you, I'll keep all the jobs to myself. I'll even stop begging you to sleep with me."

Don't be so hasty. But she clenched her teeth before those words could escape. "So what does that leave us with?"

"Each other's company," he said. "And a beautiful night to enjoy it."

"Garrison, I'm serious about this."

"I know."

Just then the waitress arrived at their table, her large silver tray heavy with the dishes they had ordered.

"Perfect timing." Garrison adjusted the glasses on the table to give her room to put the food.

He thanked the waitress with a truly pleased smile. "This looks delicious."

"Enjoy," she said. "And let me know if you need anything else." Then she turned and left them to their meal.

Before Reyna could say anything, Garrison held up a hand. His platinum cuff links flashed in the candlelight. "Truce. I don't want anything to spoil this beautiful meal. Okay?"

She had to agree. "Okay."

The food was beautifully tempting and ready to eat. Vegetable stew with Jollof rice. Chicken roti. Peanut butter and fish soup. Fried ripe plantains. Reyna spread her napkin over her lap and turned to the business of enjoying their meal.

She and Garrison ate and spoke of other things. His mother, who loved her life in Tampa. Her parents, who still lived in their first house in Trenton. Her job at the tattoo parlor.

"What would you do if I walked in and asked you for a tattoo?"

Reyna laughed, surprised. "I'd ask if you were in the right place."

The question had her eyes moving irresistibly over him. His flesh was smooth, brown and hard everywhere. Unmarked. It would be a shame to touch ink to it and spoil his perfection. She told him as much.

"But your tattoo is beautiful," he said with a smoldering look at her, as if he could see beneath the fabric of her dress to the skin he spoke so lovingly of. "It adds to the symmetry and beauty of your body. It gives me an excuse to kiss every inch of your arm, shoulder and back."

He had done just that in the dark hours of the night when they lay in his bed. With satisfaction lying low and sweet in her belly, she had felt him press delicate kisses over every part of her tattoo, down to her wrist and her fingers, then back up again. She blushed at the memory of it.

The candlelight flickering between them on the

table reminded her of the cabin at Halcyon, the way the light moved over his hands, over his face.

"Thank you," she said in response to his compliment, her skin warming with a blush.

The faintest of smiles drifted over his lips. "You're a beautiful woman, and I'm privileged to get this second chance to know you."

He sounded so sincere, so gentlemanly, that all she could do was nod her head to accept his compliment. Again. The restaurant was filling up, the diners who'd been there before they arrived leaving to make room for the night owls.

As she shared the last of her fried plantains with Garrison and told him about her parents' love story, she became vaguely aware of a low-key buzz in the restaurant, the other diners turning from their meal to face the door. She frowned at Garrison, getting ready to ask what was going on, but his attention was completely focused on her. She stumbled into his intent gaze, the words falling back from her lips.

"Finish what you were saying," he said. "I'm listening."

His voice rumbled low and deep, sending a sensual thrill through her body. She forgot what she was talking about. The plantains were sweet on her tongue, her lips slick from the light oil they had been fried in. But despite every reservation she had about Garrison, it was his taste she wanted in her mouth, his essence wetting her lips. She drew a ragged breath.

This was ridiculous. Why couldn't she keep a single coherent thought in her head? It was different, she decided, being with him in the mountains, hating him, then making love with him. It all seemed like such an anomaly, something outside her normal life and experience. Something she could safely indulge in without repercussions. But now, with him in her city, at a restaurant near her apartment, things didn't seem so safe anymore.

"Garrison Richards?"

She blinked when he tore his eyes away from hers to glance at the person who had just spoken. Reyna blinked in surprise. It was her ex-husband.

Ian looked the same as when she had seen him last time on the television screen, his white teeth bared in a polished grin, hair freshly cut and perfectly accentuating his chiseled face. Handsome. With the money he'd made from his successful TV show, he dressed well in a pair of thousand-dollar jeans, what seemed like an equally expensive shirt and a dark blazer. His terra-cotta skin glowed as if he had just come from the spa.

Ian stood near their table staring at Garrison then at her, at the flickering candlelight between them, the nearly empty wineglasses. She could see him assessing the facts of what was before him.

Reyna nodded once to acknowledge Ian then took a sip of her wine and looked away. From the corner of her eye, she saw the flex of muscle in his jaw. He hated to be ignored, but she didn't have anything to say to him. And she couldn't imagine that he had anything to say to her.

Garrison stood up, and the two men shook hands. Vivian waited just ahead of Ian and the party of four—two women and two men—with him. Like him, the men were good-looking, square-jawed types, while the two women were both extraordinarily beautiful. Each held on to one of Ian's arms, even when he had reached over to shake Garrison's hand.

"I didn't know my ex-wife was looking for advice on another divorce so soon," Ian said.

Reyna carefully put her wineglass on the table and went back to her meal, waiting for him to leave. Still standing, Garrison put one hand in his pocket and the other on the table. "She's still single and un-encumbered, as far as I know," he said.

"Ah," Ian said, as if just understanding what was going on between his ex-wife and ex-lawyer. "You're screwing her."

Reyna never understood why someone so convincing behind the camera was as transparent as glass in real life.

"That's not a very polite thing to say." Garrison's voice dropped its cordial tone and became tempered steel.

"Polite?" Ian said with a sneer anyone close by could hear. "What's not *polite* is going through your list of former clients' ex-wives to find your next date."

Reyna drew in a swift breath. The plantain she'd put in her mouth abruptly lost all its flavor.

"Your table is ready, Mr. Barbieri." Vivian drifted toward Ian, looking uncomfortable. With subtle gestures, she was trying to get his party to their table and out of the way. Already, Ian's presence in the restaurant made nearly everyone starstruck. Now he was making another kind of scene.

"What the hell did you just say to me?" Garrison growled the question, the palm he'd rested on the table now tightened into a fist.

Reyna could feel the coiled energy in him, the unfamiliar anger. She wiped her hands on her napkin and glanced at her ex-husband, keeping her voice intentionally mild. "I think it's time you went on your way, Ian. Your lady friends look hungry."

Ian grinned as if he had scored high points in a game. "Don't think you're special, Reynie. He likes them nice and used. You should check out the other ones he's been with. It's all on the internet for you to find."

Reyna winced. She always hated it when Ian called her that, and he knew it.

"Leave now before I make you walk away, Barbieri." Garrison's voice rumbled in a dangerous register.

Nervousness flared briefly in Ian's face, then he looked around him, apparently feeling safe that he was in a crowded restaurant with witnesses and maybe even friends who could back him up. "See you around, Richards. I'm sure it'll be with another used-up ex-wife."

Garrison growled low in his throat, surging toward Ian. Reyna gasped and jumped between them just in time. Around her, she heard the gasps of other patrons, the rushing conversation as more and more people wondered out loud what was going on. Camera phones pointed at them. She grabbed Garrison's arm and pressed herself against him, showing Ian her back. "Don't. He's not worth it."

"Yes, Richards. It's not worth the lawsuit." Then Ian turned and walked away, following Vivian to a table on the other side of the restaurant.

Reyna could feel the anger vibrating just beneath Garrison's skin. He rarely smiled, rarely laughed. This temper, too, was rare. She instinctively knew that they shouldn't stay in the restaurant any longer. Not as long as Ian was there. "We should go," she said.

"No. He's not going to drive us away from our meal."

She glanced down at the scattered remnants of their dinner, two empty plates, the half-finished bowl of plantains, the bottle of wine that still had plenty left in it. Before Ian arrived, they had been sipping their wine, snacking on the last of the plantains and allowing the conversation to begin the slow process of digestion. It was nothing they could go back to.

Reyna squeezed his forearm. It was a steel rod beneath her fingers, firm and cold. She'd never imagined the cool and calm lawyer could even get this angry.

"We should go," she said again.

Garrison watched her for a moment. Before her eyes, his face slowly settled into its usual impassive lines. He drew a breath. "All right."

After he paid the check, Reyna slipped out of the restaurant at his side with the curious stares of the other restaurant patrons at their backs. In the cold evening, he took another deep breath. The steam from his sigh smoked the air.

"Let's go for a walk," she said. "It'll clear your head."

"My head is clear enough," Garrison said gruffly, his voice not quite back to normal. But instead of heading to the car, he tucked her arm in the crook of his elbow and started down the busy sidewalk.

They walked in silence, footsteps ringing against the pavement, strolling past banks of dirty snow,

brightly lit storefronts, men loitering on the cold
street corners.

"I should apologize," he finally said. "I don't usually let people get to me like that."

"Yes, I can see how that could be a hazard at the
negotiation table."

Reyna was trying to ignore her own unease. Garrison had gotten upset out of proportion to what Ian
said. Was that because her ex's accusations were true?
Whatever the case, now didn't seem the best time to
ask about it.

Their slow footsteps took them into a less-populated
part of the neighborhood, fewer people, closed stores,
a more residential area with the wash of lights from
apartment buildings falling down on them from both
sides of the street. The sound of a television came from
a nearby window.

"Do you believe I've done what he said?"

She pressed her lips together. "It's not for me to
believe—"

"Yes, it is. Your opinion matters to me. If you think
I'd do something so...low and desperate, then that's a
conversation we need to have." He cursed, an unexpected and filthy exhalation in the cool night. "That's
not even a conversation, that's—" He cursed again
and turned to her. "I feel a bit out of my mind right
now, and I don't even know why."

She felt the strength in him, the trembling anger
that simmered beneath the seemingly rational words.
"Garrison." She touched his chest through the thick
wool coat. He pressed his gloved hand over hers.

"Reyna." His voice grated with emotion.

He looked up at the skies as if to find guidance

from some higher power, but in the silence of the evening, it was just the two of them, the streets empty of everything except their shadows. He put his arms around her and said her name again. "I don't want you to believe the worst of me."

But I don't know you. Not really. The words hovered on the tip of her tongue, but he kissed her and swallowed them. It was a hard and desperate kiss. A kiss that spoke of a deeper hunger than the flesh. Reyna gasped into his mouth, kissed him back, sparked by the desperation in his touch. He repeated her name as he kissed her. Sweetness. Heat. Desire. Then they weren't on the sidewalk anymore. An alley's wall was at her back, and he was pressing heated kisses to her throat, loosening the button at the top of her coat.

His lust frightened her. But she couldn't deny the spark of arousal between her thighs, the quickening of her breath that responded to the need in him. Her pulse swam desperately in her throat. He gripped her hips and moved against her, a hard and frantic heat. Even through their clothes, she could feel the thick proof of his desire. But she wanted more. Beyond shame, Reyna quickly unbuttoned his coat, touched him through his slacks. He groaned into her throat, pulled her hips into his, breath gasping. His gloved hands slid up her thighs, lifted her.

"Reyna…"

She was slick and hot for him, pulse thundering, her reason gone. He yanked a glove off with his teeth, slid a hand between her thighs, shoving her dress up and out of his way. She swallowed a gasp and whimpered when his long fingers stroked her, tested her readiness for him. She sucked his tongue into her mouth and clung to his shoulders. Her heart thundered as he adjusted his clothes, then hers. He plunged deep into her.

"Oh!"

He was still for a moment, breath gasping into her throat as they both got used to the hot fit of their bodies together. Then he began to move. Garrison was steadily building speed and heat, the perfect hammer of lust. She threw her head back against the wall as he claimed her, the long wings of his coat protecting her flesh from anyone's sight but his own.

He grunted softly with each movement of his body. She bit her lips together to stifle her moans, though the firm stroke of him inside her made her want to scream at the moon, howl at the stars.

The pleasure crawled up inside Reyna, twisting savagely in her belly. She clawed at his back through the coat, moving with him, as desperate for satisfaction as he was. He groaned as he achieved his peak, shuddering and whispering her name. Garrison threw his head back, panting breaths misting the air. She squirmed, her pleasure still unfulfilled. Reyna whimpered with loss when Garrison pulled his body from hers. But he put a hand between them, sliding his fingers over the firm seed of her passion, into her wetness. His fingers teased, circled, blazing up her banked fires.

Her palms slapped the wall. Her hips moved, blindly seeking. Her breath grew labored.

"Oh, God!"

Cold air washed over her stockinged legs, between her thighs where his fingers were merciless, twisting the pleasure inside her. She writhed against the wall, caught between the cold brick and the relentless press and caress of his fingers, the wet pleasure of it. His face was intent and hard, a fierce beauty blazing in him as he plunged between her legs again and again with his fingers. She exploded with bliss.

Reyna flung her back off the wall, crying out his name and panting into the night. She gasped and sagged into him, desperately clutching him as the last tremors took her body. He held her to him, his hot breath searing her throat.

"I'm sorry." He panted. "I didn't mean for that to happen."

But what held more weight was the fulfilled promise of his desire for her, the satisfaction that was warm and pulsing at the top of her thighs and low in her belly. It felt sinful and wild. She'd never done anything like this before, made love in public, abandoned caution and allowed her body's wants to rule her. She couldn't quite obey her common sense that told her to pull away, pull her skirt down and go home.

Slowly, he released her to the ground on unsteady feet. He pulled her close, still not speaking. Which was fine with her because she had no idea what to say. His anger was gone. In its place was a resolute silence that oddly comforted her. At his car, he opened the door for her, then he got in. They drove out of the small neighborhood. She didn't realize until a long while later that they were traveling across the Brooklyn Bridge toward Manhattan.

"Where are we going?"

"Back to my place. I hope you don't mind. I

thought it would be better instead of just dropping you off at home, after…" He didn't need to say after what.

Reyna blushed and turned from him to look out the window. She was still tingling, still deliciously aware of everything she'd done with him. And she didn't have a single regret.

Garrison lived in an apartment near Central Park. They swept past a doorman who greeted them with a respectful nod before going back to his business with the weekend newspaper. An elevator carried them swiftly to the twenty-second floor.

Inside, the curtains were pulled open to let in the lights of the city and a view of the park, covered in darkness. Garrison pressed a button, and the recessed lighting flickered on, emphasizing the large living room's intimate darkness rather than pushing it away.

The apartment was massive and high-ceilinged, affording a corner view of the city and park through wide floor-to-ceiling windows. Bookshelves lined the walls, and heavy wooden furniture sat in an inviting arrangement. The overall effect was very masculine, very refined. Somber. But nothing she didn't expect.

Garrison took Reyna's coat and tucked it along with his own in the hall closet. He jerked off his tie and flung it over a nearby chair then gestured for her to have a seat on the leather couch. After a slight hesitation, he shed his suit jacket, too.

"Would you like a drink?"

She sank down into the dark brown couch that smelled pleasantly of leather and oak, the fabric pressing into her skin with a momentary coolness then a full-body comfort, a sumptuous invitation to release any tension and worry. It was very much like Garrison's embrace. "Red wine, if you have it."

"I do."

He poured her a glass of something full-bodied and expensive then presented the wine to her with a sort of bow, but did not sit with her on the couch. Instead, he poured himself a glass of whiskey and walked to the window. Garrison stared out into the night while he drank from the glass, obviously distracted.

Reyna took those seconds to admire him, the way the dress shirt and vest fit his wide shoulders and showed off his trim waist, the slim fit of the slacks over his rear—here, she lingered for an indecently long time—his muscular thighs and the oddly erotic bend of his knee. The night sky beyond the window framed him like a work of art. A work of art she wanted to drag to bed.

Two weeks before, she'd found him sexy and thought there was nothing beautiful about him except for his naked body. But she realized now that *all* of him *was* beautiful; his was an austere splendor that caught the viewer unawares, made them, made *her*, lose her breath, even as a hunger grew to see more of him.

She gripped the stem of her wineglass as she realized what that meant.

Well, damn.

As if he'd read her thoughts, Garrison stirred by the window. His face was actually calmer, as if he'd made peace with part of himself, even made some sort of decision while staring out at the city. "Things didn't quite work out the way I planned, Reyna."

"What had you planned, exactly?" She put her

wineglass on the table, unwilling to look too closely at
the realization that just slapped her neatly in the face.

He turned to her, the whiskey glass held loosely
in his hand. "I had romance in mind for our date,
not…not what actually happened. This date was to
prove to you that we can have more than great sex
together." The corner of his mouth tilted up in a hu-
morless smile. "Can we start the night over?"

Start over? She didn't think there was anything to
start over from. They had a great time in the mountains, and now he wanted to bring that magic into
the real world. It wouldn't work; it could only be that
animalistic craving they had shared in the alley, a different kind of magic. Raw and so intense that it hurt.

It didn't matter that she now found him beautiful,
and a piece of her heart was no longer hers.

To make time to gather her thoughts, Reyna
twirled the red wine in her glass and watched the
legs drip down the sides of the expensive crystal.
She pursed her lips.

"Let's not pretend this is more than it is." She
couldn't look at him. "The sex is great, but there's
no way this can end well. We should just cut this
short now. That way, nobody will get hurt." *Or I won't
get hurt.*

She heard the faint tap of crystal on wood and
looked up to see that he had put his glass on the bar
and now walked to her with a purposeful glint in his
eyes. He took the glass from her hand and tugged
her to her feet.

"It's not fair of you to kill this before it even gets a
chance to start." His hands were warm and big around
hers. "I want to get to know more than just how you

sound when we're making love. I know you want me. Give it a chance for there to be even more between us."

His breath, spiced from the whiskey, brushed her cheek. A shiver of lust shook her belly. *This is not the time,* she told herself. But his closeness was playing havoc with her senses. She wanted to move closer to him. The kisses they'd already shared haunted her. She was very aware that all she had to do was step a few inches closer, and those kisses would be hers again. Her eyes flickered over his shoulder, glancing toward the darkened hallway and where she assumed his bedroom was. *Damn.* Reyna stepped back.

"I think I'm way over my head here," she said.

He released her hands but stayed within touching distance. "Swim through it," he murmured, his sweepingly long lashes and ascetic face kissed with sensual decadence. "It's not so overwhelming once you allow yourself to enjoy it."

He was clearly over whatever crisis of conscience had overtaken him after their lustful encounter in the alley. She wondered at that, how it was possible to process something so quickly and get past it. Her issues had a much stronger grip.

"Garrison, things aren't that—"

Just then a cell phone rang, an urgent chiming that was too loud to ignore. Garrison gave her a look of apology and pulled the phone from his pocket. He frowned at the display. "Damn. I've got to take this. I'll be right back. If you need to freshen up, the guest bedroom and bath are down that hallway." He pointed where she had glanced before then headed toward the hallway on the other side of the living room, lifting the phone to his ear. His voice switched from the intimate tones she was used to, became harder and businesslike. "Tell me something I want to hear," he said.

His deep voice rumbled, gradually becoming indecipherable sounds as he disappeared down the hallway and through a nearby door.

Damn. What was she doing? Hours ago, she was determined never to see him again, but now all she wanted was to get naked and rub herself all over him through that gorgeous suit. She wasn't thinking with her brain.

He was like no man she had ever even thought of becoming involved with. He was no artist, no sensitive and passionate soul. Instead, he was a businessman with a cool and rational mind that sometimes chilled her with its precision. If there was a problem, he often had a solution—not a nice one, but one that was workable.

At the restaurant, even in the midst of his anger, she had seen him calculate the benefits and drawbacks of beating the hell out of Ian in front of everyone. She was sure that if she hadn't stopped him, he would have stopped himself. She didn't know him completely, but she liked to think she was beginning to.

Reyna left her wine on the coffee table to find the bathroom. When Garrison mentioned freshening up, she realized she still felt sticky from their encounter in the alley.

When she finished, Garrison was still on the phone. To occupy herself, she wandered around the large living room.

Now that she didn't have Garrison's hypnotic presence to distract her, she noticed that his apartment reminded her of Bridget's place on the other side of the park. It was smaller than her friend's multimillion-dollar, two-story penthouse, but the view was just as dizzying, the furnishings more impeccable and with an international flair.

A pair of African birthing chairs took up queenly space near the large and neatly arranged bookshelves. A Turkish rug lay underfoot, and a heavy, wooden screen with Adinkra symbols carved into it separated the reading area from the rest of the room.

Reyna stood near the screen to read the symbols, trying to remember what she learned from the class on West African culture and language she took her junior year. As she stretched to examine the images carved into the screen, her hip nudged a folder sitting on top of a nearby table. She hissed as the folder fell, scattering papers onto the floor.

With a curse, she bent to pick them up, gathering them quickly in some semblance of order to slide them back into the manila folder. A name on top of one of the documents caught her eye. She blinked. No, it couldn't be. Before she caught herself, she was tugging the document free of the folder again to look at it properly.

The breath left her throat in a shocked rush. Reyna felt as if she had been kicked in the stomach.

At the top of the heavy white sheet of paper, clean and freshly printed, was Marceline's name, and the husband she was filing divorce from. Garrison was the lawyer representing Marceline's husband. She dropped the paper as if it burned. And in some ways, it did. A hot, scorching thing sat in the center of her chest, eating away at the soft feelings she had for Garrison. She felt betrayed.

Had his appearance at Halcyon simply been a ploy to get close to Marceline and find out anything that her husband could use against her? Had he been gathering information on her friend that entire time? A fluttering noise jerked Reyna from her thoughts, the manila folder falling again to her feet. She stared at the innocuous-looking folder then picked it up, shoved the papers back inside and put it back on the desk.

Her fingers shook, and cold horror settled in the pit of her belly. This wasn't possible. But she couldn't ignore the damning evidence in front of her face. Reyna grabbed her purse and coat. She yanked open the front door.

"My apologies. That took much longer than I thought it would."

Garrison came back into the living room, slipping the phone back into his pocket. He stopped short when he saw her at the door wearing her coat. "You're leaving?"

"You bastard!" Reyna spat. "How could you do this to me? To her?"

"What are you talking about?" He walked toward her, hands held up in a posture of surrender. "Come sit down so we can talk about whatever is bothering you."

She struggled to button her coat, the anger making her fingers slip. "No more games, Garrison! I will not give you the chance to snowball me again."

"I'm really in the dark here. Reyna, what's wrong?"

"Don't you dare say my name. Not like that." She cursed the trembling weakness in her voice and backed away from him as he moved cautiously closer. "Did you know that Marceline was your client's wife the whole time, or did you find out and decide to use it to your advantage later on?"

An eyebrow rose. "Marceline? Your friend?"

"Yes!" Her voice rose in a scream. "You are her husband's lawyer. Daniel Keller. How convenient for you to forget to tell me."

"Keller's wife is not Marceline. It's Brigitte."

Reyna stared at him coldly, trying to control her temper as someone passing by the open door stopped to look at her before rushing past to the elevator. "Brigitte M. Keller. She uses her middle name with us because we already have a Bridget."

Garrison stopped. An emotion moved quickly across his face, too fast for Reyna to see. He stood in the wide hallway, maddeningly cool in his suit despite the discarded jacket and tie. A frown creased his brow.

"I didn't know any of that," he said. "Keller always referred to his wife as Brigitte."

"And you expect me to believe someone like you isn't thorough enough to know that simple damn fact?" She blinked back tears of anger. "If you lie so easily about this, you could have damn well lied to me about sleeping with other ex-wives of your old clients."

Garrison stiffened. Whatever emotion she had sensed in him before drained away. He watched her with a coldness that made her want to gather her coat more closely around her. "Do you really believe that?" he asked.

She swallowed, glancing back toward the papers

with her friend's name. "Right now I don't know what to believe." Reyna walked out of the apartment and closed the door behind her.

The elevator came quickly, and in just a few minutes she was downstairs in the cold and slush, rushing toward the subway station in her impractical heels. She felt chilled and could not get warm enough, but it had nothing to do with the weather. She trembled the entire way home.

Chapter 10

Garrison stood frozen in the middle of his living room, wondering what the hell just happened. One moment, he was planning one of the most romantic nights of his life, arranging for his favorite restaurant in the city to send them dessert along with a bottle of wine, and the next...the next, Reyna was raving at him about something he had no idea about. A stupid coincidence. Then she had thrown *that* accusation at him. And it hurt.

When Barbieri said it at the restaurant, Garrison had been furious. That piece of nothing didn't know him, yet he *dared* hint that Reyna was some piece of castoff Garrison had gotten from another man's trash. She was much more than that. And Garrison was, too.

His business was his life. He had built it from the ground up with no capital invested from a wealthy parent, no business connections except the ones he'd forged in New York on his own. Nothing. Garrison Richards and Associates was something he'd built with his two hands and his reputation.

His law firm supported his mother, helped her to leave the workforce and live the life she'd always dreamed of. This was what paid for every morsel of food that went into Garrison's mouth. He would never, *ever* think of endangering it just to find someone to warm his bed.

But Reyna thought he would. What had he ever done to make her believe he was a conscienceless opportunist who preyed on vulnerable women?

He breathed through the tightness in his chest. She was gone.

Garrison shook himself and grabbed his keys, his coat. He couldn't let her leave. And the high heels she wore didn't seem suited for the slush that sat in haphazard piles all over the city. He ran downstairs to look for her, thought he saw her fleeing down into the subway, but by the time he crossed the street and ran down the steps, the train to Brooklyn was only a howling sound and brace of wind blowing back at him in the tunnel.

Garrison cursed. His coat flapped around his legs in the wake of the southbound train. He glanced at his watch, mentally calculating how long it would take her to get home. He got his car and drove toward her Brooklyn apartment as fast as the streets would let him.

He parked on the street across from the subway exit closest to her building and waited. Barely ten minutes later, he breathed a sigh of relief when he saw her familiar figure emerge from the subway station. She was huddled in her coat, the long material covering her from throat to calves. She walked quickly from the station, a slim and dark figure, checking her surroundings as she made her way from the well-lit entrance. Even covered as she was, the swaying walk of hers managed to attract quite a few admirers. Garrison got out of his car.

"Reyna."

She stopped when she saw him. Her hands were stuffed in her pockets, and she looked as if she was freezing. "What are you doing here?"

"I was worried about you."

"I'm obviously fine." She began to walk again, her heels stabbing into the sidewalk with each deliberate step. She stopped at the red-lit pedestrian crossing. "You can go back home now."

Garrison gently took her arm, his gloved hand against her black sleeve. "Let me drive you home."

She looked down at his hand as if it was something loathsome. "I walk these streets every day. I am fine. I don't need your fake chivalry, and I definitely don't need you to tell me when I'm safe and when I'm not." Reyna yanked her arm from his. "The only time I wasn't safe was when you took advantage of my friend and used me to get to her."

Garrison flinched, but he tried not to show how deeply her words pierced him, a shocking arrow of pain in his chest that he'd never felt before. He drew back. "All right."

The light changed, and she quickly crossed the street, nearly lost in the swarm of pedestrians. She didn't look back. But Garrison followed her the whole way home to make sure she was as safe as she thought she was. At her building, she walked inside and slammed the door in his face without once looking in his direction. Garrison went back to his car. He cursed when he saw the parking ticket on the windshield. Of course this would happen.

But when he got into the Jag and started the engine, he couldn't find the energy to be angry about the fine. He had parked where he shouldn't. Fair enough. What wasn't fair were her accusations of duplicity.

But life isn't quite fair, is it?

Garrison wanted to kick his inner sardonic voice in the throat. He tightened his fists around the steering wheel. His leather gloves creaked.

At Halcyon, he thought he'd shown Reyna the kind of man he was. The oblivious and morally blind man from five years ago had been burned away by his own deliberate fires of change. Now he was more conscious of the people who could be hurt by his actions. And he changed lives for the better when he could. Garrison thought that was the man she'd responded to and made love with in the mountains.

The person she had allowed to touch her would have never done those things she so freely accused him of. Why, then, did she think it was possible for him, now that they were back in the city, to do those despicable things? Garrison shook his head. It was not a question he could answer.

Resigned, he pulled the car into traffic and headed for the bridge.

At home, he poured himself another whiskey then carefully checked his notes on the Keller divorce.

As he read the details, he remembered what he had seen of the young Haitian woman at the resort. She was beautiful and gentle, but with an air of sadness about her, as if depression was only a breath away. She looked like someone who had lost at love and lost badly.

The man who wanted to be her ex-husband was doing much better. Although Daniel Keller often talked about how he missed his wife and wished things would go back to how they once were, he did not wear anguish the way Marceline did. But that wasn't surprising.

For the men who came to him—"the shark lawyer"—for an effective and incisive divorce, all the soft feelings and tenderness for the women who had shared their lives were long gone. All that was left was a desire for self- and asset preservation.

It was a depressing scenario, one that Garrison told himself he had been lucky to escape. Nothing ended in happiness. And those who were fools to forget that were the ones who suffered the most.

Chapter 11

Reyna rushed into her apartment and locked the door. The cold night air had burned into her lungs, freezing them as she'd breathed openmouthed, pushing tears of disappointment and anger at bay, on her walk from Garrison's apartment and then from the subway station. Her nose stung with cold. She still couldn't believe she'd allowed herself to fall for his brand of bull. And almost fall for him.

She dropped her purse on the coffee table, kicked off her shoes and sank into the couch.

"I'm such an idiot."

Before she could start crying, she grabbed her cell phone and quickly dialed a number. Louisa answered on the second ring.

"What are you up to, girl? I thought you'd be too busy getting pounded into the mattress to call me at this hour."

The tears Reyna fought so long against rushed down her face. "He's a liar, Louisa."

"What? He's a lawyer? I thought we all knew that."

She sniffled, smiling weakly at her friend's joke. She bit her lip and told her what happened at his apartment.

"Did you sleep with him again? Before?"

Reyna toyed with the necklace at her throat, blushing as if Louisa could see her. "Yes." And she would have slept with him again if she hadn't found those papers with Marceline's name on them.

"You must really like him."

"I did," Reyna muttered. "I must be a fool."

"Stop being so hard on yourself. He's a sexy man with enough appeal to make any woman forget her common sense. And although you're not any woman, you're not immune to the appeal of a fine man, no matter what you tell yourself." The faint rustle of fabric came through the phone, the sigh of a mattress. Was Louisa in bed?

"Are you home?"

"No, I'm not. But I will be tomorrow."

"Oh, my God, I'm sorry. I didn't mean to interrupt your night. I feel like such an idiot!"

"Stop beating yourself up, honey. It gets old. If I didn't want to talk with you, I wouldn't have answered the phone."

"I still feel bad." Reyna took a deep breath and wiped the tears away with trembling fingers. "I'm going to take a long bath and get myself together. You enjoy the rest of your night. Okay?"

"Reyna…"

"No, really. Please." She took her cell phone from

her ear to look at the clock. "This is so booty call hour—what was I thinking?"

"You were thinking that you need a friend, and that is exactly what I am."

"I know. Thank you for answering my call." She forced a smile into her voice. "Now I'm going to be a friend to you and hang up so you can go back to whoever you're entertaining right now. I'm sure he'd appreciate it. Good night, Louisa."

Her friend sighed. "Fine. But let's meet up tomorrow. We can have brunch at our usual place then go see Marceline. I already know she doesn't feel like going out, so we'll just have to go to her."

"That sounds good," Reyna said softly. "See you tomorrow."

She disconnected the call and lay down on the rug, curled onto her side with a fist under her cheek. A sigh shook her body from head to toe. That sigh became a sob, then fresh tears fell.

Yes, she thought as she tasted the salt from her eyes. *You are a fool.*

The next day when she met up with Louisa, she had herself a little more together. But as they sat down at the table for two at their favorite street-side bistro, Louisa frowned at her, her bright gaze missing nothing.

"Girl, you look a mess. Are you sure you're not going through all this for no damn good reason?"

Reyna reached for the menu, deliberately not looking at her friend. "I'm not ready to talk about this yet."

Louisa signaled their waiter. "That's fine for now, but I need the details from you *very* soon."

Reyna didn't say anything. At least not then. But by the end of brunch, Louisa had gotten every single detail from her, even the ill-advised but infinitely pleasurable detour they'd taken in the secluded alley. Louisa wasn't shocked by any of it, but she had been amused.

"Whatever else happens between you and this lawyer, at least you can say he opened up your horizons," Louisa murmured. "As well as a few other things."

Reyna nearly choked on her water.

After brunch, they left the relative noise and bustle of SoHo for the house in Long Island that Marceline had shared with her husband. Instead of taking the train, which was Reyna's usual and preferred means of transportation, Louisa insisted on driving.

As they pulled into the driveway of the massive house, Reyna noticed an unfamiliar car close to the house. A black Lamborghini.

"Is that Daniel's car?"

"I'm not sure. Maybe Marceline found herself a new beau in the past few days while we've been worried sick about her." Louisa raised an amused eyebrow as she climbed from the driver's seat of the white Mercedes. "Come on, let's go see what our bereaved friend is up to."

Reyna firmly closed the passenger-side door and walked with Louisa toward the lakeside Georgian-style mansion. The house was all white columns and wide windows with lots of beautiful landscaping that took a small army to maintain.

"She's *got* to get rid of this albatross before the divorce. What—"

Reyna broke off when angry footsteps pounded

against the stone walkway leading from the house. Daniel burst down the path toward them, barely sparing her and Louisa a glance before jumping in his car and peeling away in a screech of tires.

"What the hell?" Louisa said.

The two women hurried to the house. They didn't have to go very far before they saw Marceline slumped over the living room couch, crying as if her heart was breaking.

Reyna rushed to her side. "Honey, what's wrong?"

"What did that loser do now?" Louisa followed at a more sedate pace, her narrowed eyes taking in the neatly ordered living room as if searching for signs of something worse. Blood on the floor, a knife tucked into the potted plant, something.

"It's Daniel!" Marceline grabbed the front of Reyna's blouse. She looked shattered.

"I think we were able to figure out at least that much," Louisa said drily. But the look of concern on her face belied her tone.

Reyna made a shushing motion in her direction. "What happened?" she asked Marceline.

But her friend couldn't speak. Reyna and Louisa guided her from the living room to the kitchen, where Louisa put on water for tea. Reyna sat with her arm around Marceline at the dining room table, the large and opulent room a big contrast to the cozy space they'd shared at Halcyon.

"Tell us what's wrong, honey." Reyna smoothed her friend's hair. "If we don't know, we can't help you."

Only when Louisa returned with cups of chamomile tea did Marceline try to speak. It was probably to appease the firm look on Louisa's face, the look that said she was tired of not getting any output other than tears. Marceline stuttered a few words before going quiet again.

"It's okay." Reyna rubbed Marceline's back, murmuring softly to calm her.

With her tea in hand, Louisa strolled to the window and looked over the small vegetable garden Marceline insisted on planting despite the inhospitable New York weather. "Do I have to go find Daniel and drag him back here to find out what happened?" she finally asked.

Marceline looked terrified. "No!"

She reached for Reyna with cold hands. "He..." She swallowed. "He says he's going to yank my whole life from under me." Tears splashed down her cheeks. "He says he'll make your divorce from Ian look like Woodstock in comparison." Her chin shook as she spoke. "I can't believe this. I thought he was the one. I thought he loved me." She trembled in Reyna's arms while Reyna tried to push her own anger aside. This was about Marceline, not about her. But dammit, how dare he use what happened to her all those years ago to threaten her friend?

"This proves that he has no love for you, Marceline," Reyna said quietly. "You have to do something about this before it gets any worse. You need your own lawyer."

"No..." Marceline's weak voice suddenly grated on Reyna's nerves, reminding her too much of herself years ago.

"Snap out of it," Louisa muttered, her lips pursed

at the edge of her teacup. "What are you waiting for? For him to punch your lights out?"

Marceline froze in Reyna's arms. Reyna drew a breath, sharp and surprised. *No,* she thought, *not this.* Louisa was at their side in seconds.

She stared at Marceline. "He hit you before?"

"Yes, but…"

"No." Louisa sharply cut her off. She abandoned her tea on the table, hands visibly trembling. "Reyna. We need to take care of this. Now."

We? Reyna's mind raced. What could she do to help Marceline? She didn't have the clout that Bridget and her parents had, nor the financial resources available to Louisa. Marceline's parents had been wealthy but died leaving her orphaned, if exceedingly rich. She was alone with no remaining family in the United States. No one to turn to except her friends. And all Reyna had to offer her, as a friend, was Garrison.

Chapter 12

Garrison sat behind his desk with his legs stretched out, his eyes closed. The day had been a long one, client after client, a few conferences, until finally, now at six in the evening, the tempo of the office was getting lower, business falling to a gentle hum instead of the usual frantic buzz.

He sat in his dress shirt, sleeves rolled up to the elbows, his suit jacket long discarded after his last meeting. The small, powerful heater he kept in his office—in addition to the one that warmed the entire suite—hummed quietly nearby. Anthea was getting ready to leave, the other three attorneys who worked for him were already gone and the cleaning staff was about to come through.

This was the lull before his rush of evening work. The moment when everything he had been fighting off mentally threatened to overwhelm him. And thoughts of *her* overwhelmed him. The smiling tease of her face in the candlelight. The way she looked down, long lashes brushing her cheeks like luxurious silk fans, just before she challenged him on something.

Reyna floated just beneath his consciousness, beautiful and angry, an avenging angel. Was it wrong that the fierceness of her, the protective instinct that had made her snap and snarl at him, also made him want her even more?

His cell phone rang, pulling him from his thoughts. He picked up the call after a brief glance at the display.

"Wolfe. What a nice surprise."

He turned around in his chair to face the window, his smile automatic at hearing from his good friend from college. The setting sun warmed his face, and he squinted from its brightness.

"You sure I'm not interrupting some wild office party up there?" Wolfe asked with the usual laughter in his voice.

Garrison didn't bother to ask his friend how he knew he was still in the office long after five o'clock.

"Of course you're interrupting something. You know me." He tipped back in the chair to take in the haloed view of Manhattan, the Chrysler Building and the striking power of the city he never got tired of. "There's a stripper giving me a lap dance as we speak."

"Damn!" Wolfe laughed outright. "I better hurry up and get to the point so you can return to your fun."

Garrison chuckled. "What's going on?"

"I'm heading up your way for a meeting in a few months. I figure I better give you some notice, otherwise you'd be locked up in your usual monastic solitude, unable to make time for an old friend."

"Let me know the exact date, and I'll put you on my calendar." He was only joking a little. "You need a place to stay?"

"No. Not officially. I'll be in town with Nichelle." Wolfe named his business partner and longtime friend. "But if you ply me with that expensive scotch of yours, I might have to crash in your guest bedroom at least one night."

"You know you're always welcome."

Wolfe was a friend he'd made in college, an ebullient and charismatic man who attracted women the way flowers drew bees. Many of these women wondered out loud and to Garrison's face what someone like Wolfe, a brilliant jock, was doing with a friend like Garrison, who was brilliant, too, but more reserved in his interaction with women and everyone else on campus. They met the first week at Columbia and had been in each other's lives since.

"Good to know some things never change." Wolfe chuckled.

The intercom button on Garrison's office phone buzzed. He sat up. "Hey, I have to take this call."

"Sure," Wolfe said. "I'll call you again later on in the week."

"All right." He hung up his cell phone. "Yes, Anthea?"

"You have a Miss Allen here to see you. She doesn't have an appointment but insists you'll see her anyway."

Garrison sat up. Reyna? Or was this some annoying coincidence, just like the situation with Reyna's best friend being the wife of one of his clients? "What is this woman's full name?"

His secretary tilted her mouth from the phone to ask. The answer she came back with settled a mixture of chagrin and satisfaction in his belly. "Send her in. And you can head out now. No need for you to stay longer than necessary."

He heard the barely repressed curiosity in Anthea's voice. "Of course, Mr. Richards." In the morning she would—very subtly, of course—give him the third degree.

A few seconds later, Reyna walked into his office. The sight of her was like a shot to the solar plexus. Garrison had to actually steady himself against his desk when he stood up to greet her. She was breathtaking in her low-heeled boots, tight black jeans and hip-length red jacket. Her hair was pulled back from her face in a severe style that suited the dark red lips and dramatic eyeliner. She looked armored and ready for battle.

Reyna adjusted the messenger bag over her shoulder. She was restless, unease dancing beneath the calm on her face. That haunted look made him want to stroke her back until she relaxed, and she looked at him with that familiar melting that he always had to work hard for. But he didn't touch her.

"This is a surprise," he said. "What brings you here?"

She licked her lips. "Can I sit down?"

"Of course." He waved her to the couch then sat. The tension in her reminded him of how she had been in the mountains when Marceline went missing. It seemed like an anxiety that had nothing to do with her, but rather with someone she cared deeply for. She adjusted the messenger bag around her shoulders then took it off, dropped it on the couch and shoved up the sleeves of her jacket.

He thought briefly of turning off his heater so she could be more comfortable then immediately dismissed the idea. She wouldn't stay long enough for it to make a difference.

"Is this about Marceline?"

She looked up at him in surprise. Her white teeth sank into the full nutmeg pink of her lips. "How did you know?"

He sat and waited while she gathered herself, apparently deciding what and how much to tell him. When she still didn't speak, he went to the bar tucked away near the far wall and made her some hot chocolate. She smiled tightly at him in thanks when he handed it to her. She put the mug to her lips and sighed into the steam that billowed up around her face. Her red lips stained the white mug.

She sipped in silence. He waited. If she was in no hurry, then he wasn't, either. Garrison breathed quietly, bathing in the softness of her presence in his office, an office that had only seen hard things and catered to dreadful business. He loved that she was there, marking his physical space the way she had carved a space for herself in his head. He couldn't uproot her if he tried.

"Marceline's husband is an abuser."

He jerked himself from his hazy thoughts of Reyna and the places she could fit in his life. "Excuse me?"

"Daniel Keller beats on her like they're in a damn fight club."

Garrison held himself still. "You're absolutely sure?"

"I am sure," Reyna said. "She told me." Despite the subject matter, she was calm, as if she'd practiced saying the words to him without shouting. Or crying. She cradled the hot chocolate just below her nose before tasting it.

He braced his forearms against his thighs. "Tell me."

She drew a deep breath and told him about the scene she and Louisa had stumbled into. Daniel Keller rushing out and leaving behind a devastated Marceline. She and Louisa talking to their friend and hearing the details of the emotional and physical abuse she'd endured from Keller. By the time she finished, Garrison was ready to call the cops himself. It was always the laughing ones. The ones you didn't suspect. There was nothing about Keller that said he was overaggressive, was compensating for something or wanted a regular human punching bag.

Then again, the relationship he had with Garrison was strictly business. He was handling the athlete's divorce, and Keller was paying him. They never socialized. Keller never invited him to any games or private parties with the Giants. He was simply not a man whom Garrison connected with at all. Perhaps this had something to do with it.

Garrison stood up. "I'll call Keller and tell him I can't represent him anymore."

That was the least of what he wanted to do. Hearing what the woman had been through—and he was

sure she had sanitized some of it for his benefit—
made him want to do something permanently dam-
aging to Keller. What gave him the right to treat a
woman like that? A woman he claimed to have once
loved.

Reyna looked surprised. She held the mug of hot
chocolate in her lap, her hands curled around the handle as if it alone would anchor her to the couch instead of wherever it was her mind had wandered to
minutes before.

Her lips parted. "You don't have to do that."

"Yes, I do." He didn't bother telling her about his
mother and the abusive boyfriend she'd had while
Garrison was in high school. Those two years made
him vow that Marian Richards would never have to
rely on any lover for anything else. "I cannot work
with a man who mistreats women."

Reyna's nod of satisfaction, a confirmation perhaps of something she already knew, warmed him.
But he focused on the matter at hand.

"Does Marceline have a lawyer of her own?"

Reyna's head dipped. She almost looked…embar-
rassed. "No. She never got one. She was hoping that
he'd just come to his senses and come back home
to her."

Just as Reyna once had, Garrison thought with
sudden understanding. He had not been able to help
Reyna then, but he would do what he could to make
Marceline's situation better.

He took a card from his desk and passed it to her.
Their fingertips brushed, a single electric touch.

"Give this to Marceline. Tell her she can call me

anytime about the divorce. The arrangement Keller and I had should be dissolved by morning."

"That quickly?" She seemed pleased, hopeful.

"I don't like to waste time." Garrison gave her a meaningful look.

The sun had crept through the window to touch her while they talked. It made her glow in her austere red and black, her beauty seductive and irresistible. His want for her overwhelmed him suddenly. Not just for her body, but to have her in his life, despite everything that had passed between them.

Reyna nibbled on her lip and put down her half-finished drink. "Okay, I should go." She picked up her bag and stood. "Thank you for listening. I didn't expect you to…to be so responsive, but that just shows that I don't really know you at all." She put her hands in her pockets again, eyes on his face, an irresolution to her stance. She seemed to be waiting for something. When she didn't get whatever it was, she turned from him with the barest of sighs. "I'll see you around."

She moved quickly, slipping from the couch to the door before Garrison could tell her to wait or stay or anything. His brain uncharacteristically sluggish, he escorted her to the door while the words of a dinner invitation hovered on his lips.

Reyna paused in the open doorway of his office. "You should have dinner with me tonight."

He kept his face deliberately expressionless in the wake of *his* words falling from *her* mouth.

"Why?" he asked. "Why do you want to have dinner with me?" Was it because he offered to help out her friend? He wasn't in the mood for a gratitude meal, or whatever would happen between them afterward.

Reyna seemed startled, then embarrassed, subtle color touching her cheeks.

"You don't have to repay me for this." He made a gesture that encompassed their recent conversation, the things he had promised to do for his own peace of mind.

That was the wrong thing to say because the look on her face changed from embarrassment to anger, her eyes snapping a dark fire. His fingers twitched from the urge to touch her.

"Never mind." She muttered something else and stepped out into the hallway, over to the elevators.

For a moment, he was frozen by her abrupt exit, blinking in the afterimage of her flight, the flicker of anger—or had it been chagrin?—on her face. Although she had never been difficult to read, at times he felt as if he was drowning in her emotions, inundated with so much of it that the separate feelings coming from her were difficult to sort out. The silken caress of her arousal. The vicious barbs of her anger. The rough and tender parts of her curiosity about him. In the past half hour, he'd felt all three from her, and more.

Garrison had never been a very emotional man, certainly not as much as he wanted to be. Growing up, his mother's constant emotional roller coaster made him leery of expressing even the most basic of emotions with anyone not close to him. And he had somehow cut himself off from knowing what those emotions truly meant. He'd known women who cried from practically anything. A bad movie. Broken bottles of expensive wine. Simultaneous orgasms. The same physiological reaction to such vastly different things. It frustrated him to even *begin* figuring them out.

But Reyna made him want to try.

Garrison blinked, suddenly aware that he had been staring for much too long at the empty space Reyna left. He started after her.

But when he got to the elevator, the doors were already closed. Reyna had walked away from him again.

Chapter 13

Reyna had never felt so embarrassed in her life. Garrison had dismissed her and her dinner offer as if he was absolutely done with her. Her chin wobbled, but she drew a deep breath to calm herself.

He looked so *good* in his office. That pale blue, pinstripe suit minus the jacket, his rolled-up sleeves. She had wanted to slip her arms around his waist and inhale him. Not only did he look good, he was good to her and to Marceline, too, proving himself to be essentially the polar opposite of what she had accused him of over a week ago.

Her quest to find the truth of what Ian said about Garrison and the ex-wives of his former clients yielded nothing. All she found online about Garrison was his successful law practice that catered mostly to the rich and famous, various awards for apparently being one of the sharpest legal minds in the country and a long-ago social item about a Fortune 500 CEO who'd famously offered to throw his mistress in as part of the divorce settlement Garrison was negotiating.

Reyna called herself an idiot many times over. Why had she even listened to Ian when he spouted off about the supposed other women Garrison dated? He was a compulsive liar. Hadn't she learned that lesson enough times in the past?

In the elevator, Reyna crossed her arms tightly over her chest and stared sightlessly at her reflection in the mirrored doors. There were apparently some lessons she had to learn more than once.

A few days later, Marceline called to let her know Garrison had been in touch with her, had offered her legal representation free of charge, and she was certain she could get her divorce finalized within six months. Her friend sounded stronger on the phone and animated in a way that Reyna hadn't heard in a long time. Was that Garrison's doing?

True to his word, Garrison got Marceline the divorce she wanted, and without ever having to see Daniel Keller across the negotiating table. Under the threat of his abuse of Marceline being reported to the newspapers, and his public image being ruined— although Reyna was sure it was only a matter of time before TMZ found the police report—he acquiesced to everything Garrison demanded on Marceline's behalf.

On the day the divorce became final, Reyna and the girls took Marceline to a bar in the East Village.

There, they ordered drinks, celebrated and cried with Marceline until their friend was laughing again.

Even after three months, Reyna was still horrified that her friend had been in an abusive relationship and actually wanted to stay married to her abuser. It was dreadful. And Marceline had seemed so very happy in the beginning of it all. Ecstatic. She had dared to reach for a superior love, only to be rudely awakened by a dizzying and disorienting fall.

"To Marceline!" Bridget, already drunk from her two chocolate martinis, raised her voice above the music and loud conversations in the bar. "We love you, honey baby. And any man who doesn't love you the way you deserve can kiss my butt!"

Reyna and Louisa laughed and raised their own glasses. "We'll drink to that!"

But even with her friends' cheerfulness and the half dozen cocktails she drank, Reyna found her mind still thinking about the end of Marceline's relationship, and the aborted fling she'd had with Garrison.

"Penny for your thoughts, girl."

Naturally, it was Louisa who noticed her distraction. Sitting diagonally across from Reyna at the table for four, she said the words in an absence of privacy, inviting the other women into the conversation.

"What's up, baby?" Bridget sipped her martini and looked at Reyna over her half-empty glass.

Reyna brushed the curls from her face and reached for the latest drink Bridget ordered for her. Her world was delightfully blurry. "Nothing I want to talk about right now," she said with a dismissive wave. "Tonight is about Marceline and her beautiful divorce." She lifted her glass. "Right, girls?"

Louisa arched her brow, letting her know she wasn't fooled by that delaying tactic. But she lifted her apple martini and tapped it gently against Reyna's glass. "To freedom," she said with an ironic smile.

Chapter 14

After months of nonstop work, Garrison was exhausted. Normally, that much concentration on the firm wouldn't bother him. But there were days when he had to work extra hard just to keep his head in the game. Reyna had wrapped around his consciousness like a silken vise. Even after three months, he couldn't get her out of his thoughts.

In their time apart, they had only talked through Marceline, passing cordial messages back and forth. Once, they even spoke on the telephone at her friend's insistence. Reyna was like a drug, and he was suffering through a bad case of withdrawal.

He walked into The Newsboy, a speakeasy-style bar in Chelsea that was one of Wolfe's favorite places. Even wearing his three-piece suit, he felt right at home in the bar with its exposed brick walls, deca-

dent and dark decor, and sumptuous scrolled ceiling
that looked like finely etched bronze. The bar's clien-
tele was casual, business and everything in between.

The place was packed, a line of chatting customers
at the bar, the booths with the low miniature chande-
liers and tea lights flickering on the tables. For all the
people there, it still felt warm and intimate. Probably
one of the main reasons his friend liked it so much.
After a quick look around, he easily noticed Wolfe
at a back table, his shaved head gleaming under the
low lights of the bar, teeth flashing white against his
chestnut skin and neatly trimmed goatee.

He already had a drink in front of him and a
woman perched at his shoulder. She was obviously
a stranger, but seemed to want their acquaintance to
deepen before the night was through. As Garrison
walked closer, Wolfe noticed him and said something
to the woman. By the time Garrison arrived at Wolfe's
table, she had moved on, but not before leaving behind her business card.

Wolfe stood up with a low laugh and embraced
him, patting him on the back. "You look a little tired."

"Thanks." By the time Garrison sat down, a waitress was standing near their table. She smiled flir-
tatiously at Wolfe before asking Garrison what he
wanted. He had to chuckle at his friend's ridiculous
magnetism as he gave the waitress his order then sat
back in the chair with a sigh. "Coincidentally, I *am*
a little tired."

"For you to actually admit that…" Wolfe tipped
his head, eyes smiling. "Is it a woman?"

Garrison cursed. "I've been here less than five

minutes, and you're already grilling me about my love life?"

"So it *is* a woman." Wolfe laughed. "This hasn't happened in…ever." His low chuckles drew the attention of nearly every woman nearby. "This one must be special."

"Can I at least get my drink before you start in on me?" Garrison took off his jacket and draped it across the back of the booth. He rolled up his shirt-sleeves and slowly rotated his neck until it popped once, twice.

"This girl must be doing a real number on you. Maybe you should've ordered a double."

Just then, the waitress came back with his Martinez and a refresher of what Wolfe had. "On the house," she murmured. She gave Wolfe a significant look then walked off with an excess of hip twitching.

Garrison smiled. "The burden of being you."

His friend grinned back. "I won't complain."

Garrison took a slow sip of his drink, savoring the smooth and slightly sweet cocktail of sweet vermouth and maraschino liqueur. "Speaking of a way with the ladies, where is Nichelle? I thought she was joining us tonight."

"She might. She said she ran into an old colleague in the city and wanted to spend a few hours getting reacquainted." Wolfe waved his glass in a vague gesture. "Honestly, I think she wanted to give us some time alone."

"She doesn't have to do that." Nichelle and Wolfe had known each other since they were in diapers. Their parents lived in the same neighborhood, and they had gone to pretty much the same schools until college, when she chose to go to Stanford instead of Columbia like Wolfe.

They had also pursued different graduate schools, but then Wolfe moved back to Miami to start his own business. He invited her to join him, and now it was as if they had never been apart. Garrison often wondered if there was something between them, even though Wolfe always insisted they were just friends.

"Obviously. I listen to your yammering at least once a month in one way or another." They both smiled at the joke of Garrison being a chatterbox. "Now tell me what the hell's going on so we can get back to the important stuff."

Without much more prompting, Garrison began to talk. It had been nearly a year since they last saw each other; Garrison's impromptu drive down to Tampa to see his mother had naturally led to an additional four hours on the road to visit his friend in Miami. They'd had a relaxing time at Wolfe's massive house on Fisher Island, talked about the women in their lives, what they wanted for the future, important things that were more difficult to talk about on the phone.

With the cocktail smoothing the rough edges of his day, Garrison told Wolfe everything about Reyna. When they met, the way she made him feel, his frustration with himself for not being able to make her trust him more. Until he voiced those thoughts, he hadn't quite realized how much he wanted her. And he *really* wanted her.

Years of seeing love's failures up close had jaded him. Watching his mother fall easily in and out of various disastrous relationships, then dealing with clients whose fairy-tale romances ended up as night-mares, had turned him against all kinds of love except the most temporary and physical kind. Emotionless couplings that left his body satisfied and his heart untouched. But seeing Reyna on that train changed something in him. And the weekend he spent with her had altered his worldview even more.

"Damn, man." Wolfe pointed his drink at Garrison. "Then what are you doing here? You should be at her place right now telling her how you feel."

"It doesn't work like that."

"What? Happiness? For most people, happiness is a choice, my friend." Wolfe braced his arms on the table, giving Garrison one of his rare, serious looks. "You want this woman. Hell, you obviously love her—" Garrison didn't bother denying it. "Tell her how you feel and give her the chance to deny you before you just pull yourself out of the race."

"This is not a rowing event, Wolfe." Garrison tried to laugh it off.

"Good thing, because you're a crap oarsman."

There was a gravity to Wolfe's voice that made Garrison uncomfortably aware that perhaps he had waited too long. Maybe Reyna had found someone else in the months since they'd seen each other. He knocked back his drink, anxious for the urgency in him to subside.

He never did anything in a rush. Every move he made in his life, especially important ones, he considered carefully before taking that first step. This thing with Reyna could wait. Couldn't it? Garrison's pulse tapped double time in his throat. He signaled the waitress for another drink.

It was a long time before Nichelle finally showed. She walked in with her typical elegant flair, took one look at him and Wolfe and ordered a drink for herself from a passing waitress. She attracted more than a few stares in what she had long ago adopted as a uniform. Stilettos, a figure-hugging skirt that came just below the knee and a blouse that showed off the flare of her collarbones and nothing more.

Except for the slim gold watch, everything she wore was black. With her low-cut hair and long neck, she looked like a model from a European magazine. "I see you boys really got started without me."

"We did." Wolfe made room for her at the table and rested his arm at the back of her chair.

"So what did I miss?" she asked.

"Our Garrison is going to find himself some happiness if it's the last thing he does while we're here."

Nichelle arched an elegant eyebrow and pursed her bright red lips. "Sounds intriguing. I take it this is a mission of love?"

More than halfway to being drunk, Garrison groaned. "I didn't realize I was so transparent."

Nichelle laughed. "If you were, more than half of Wolfe's conquests would be falling all over themselves to drown in your still waters. As it is..." She gestured to him, silently noting his stiffly held posture despite being quite a few sheets to the wind.

"I don't even know what that means," he muttered.

"It's okay, gorgeous. You don't have to." She made a noise of pleasure when her drink came—a dirty martini—and raised her glass in a toast. "To happiness, then?"

Chapter 15

When Reyna's doorbell rang well before noon, she expected to see Louisa on her welcome mat. But her greeting fell away when she saw Marceline's face.

"Hey, honey." They exchanged a warm hug, and Reyna invited her inside. "I'm surprised you're up this early."

"Me, too." Marceline, dressed in her usual casual-sexy style, defied the heat of summer in a light yellow sundress that set off the silken darkness of her skin. She wore her long hair twisted into a French roll. Her high heels tapped gently against the hardwood floors as she crossed the threshold. "But I wasn't so drunk last night that I didn't notice you were a little down."

She headed straight for Reyna's kitchen, poured herself a glass of lemonade and joined Reyna at the wide window seat. Reyna sipped her coffee and made room for Marceline's skinny hips. Her friend sighed and kicked off her shoes. She smiled with a touch of her old mischief when the Jimmy Choo heels clattered to the floor. She stretched and wriggled her toes. "So what's going on with you? Is it Garrison?"

Reyna sipped her warm coffee but didn't say a word. Marceline laughed.

"Don't even try that tactic with me! I've seen you use it on too many people over the years." Marceline clasped her glass of lemonade between her hands but didn't drink from it. "It's him, isn't it?"

Marceline, though one of her very best friends, wasn't someone Reyna usually talked with about romance. Marceline was someone she talked with about money, the future, how things had gotten so far off track from when they graduated high school, but for some reason the discussions of men and relationships had never been easy between them.

Reyna tipped her head back to lean into the wall and watch Marceline from beneath slightly lowered lids. It was nearly ten in the morning, and after the enthusiastic postdivorce party, she expected all her friends to be nursing hangovers in the privacy of their own homes, but Marceline looked as fresh as a beauty queen on pageant night.

Reyna was only up and sipping coffee because she had a job interview after lunch. It was with an advertising firm in the city that she'd admired for a long time. Strangely enough, it was Garrison's meddling from months before that had given her the courage to submit her application. If he thought she was good enough for Kellerman-Stark, why not a company that ranked just below them?

"Yes," she said finally. "It is him."

Marceline grinned in triumph. "I knew it. I figured it couldn't be a coincidence that the man you were lusting after at the resort is the same one helping me with my divorce for free."

Reyna vehemently shook her head, not wanting Marceline to get the wrong idea. "It's not like that."

"So you're not the reason he's helping me right now?"

"I did ask for his advice, yes, but…" She shook her head again. "Because of what happened with my divorce, I wasn't sure he was the right one to talk to."

"What does that have to do with anything, Reyna? Back then he was doing his job. Which was to get you out of Ian's life with as little trouble and expense as possible."

In that moment, Reyna regretted giving Marceline the full story of how she met Garrison. Her friend stared into her glass of lemonade, apparently caught up in something that had snagged her attention and would not let go. "He's a good man."

Reyna bit her lip. "I know," she said softly.

"Are you sure you know?" Marceline cradled her untouched lemonade in her lap and stretched out a leg toward Reyna. "If you know, then why are you moping around this apartment?"

"I'm not moping. I have an interview downtown this afternoon."

"And that's why you're sitting around here in your pajamas drinking coffee as if you had all the time in the world?" Marceline finally put the glass to her lips and took a long swallow. Traces of the lemonade dampened the fine hairs above her lip. "If you really knew what kind of man Garrison was, you would be in his office right now, kissing his face and confessing how much you miss him."

"Miss him?" It seemed a mild word for the irrational craving she had to see him, the sadness that permeated her days, even after all these months.

"Yes. You do. Don't even bother denying it."

Marceline stared down into her cup again. The confidence that blew her into Reyna's apartment suddenly wavered, showing the facade that it was. She was better, but not as well as the sunny dress, freshly done hair and smiles would indicate. Marceline drew a breath.

"Did you know that Garrison always does pro bono work for battered women?"

Reyna sat up straight. "No. I didn't." This was the first time Marceline had ever mentioned abused women; before, she always skirted any hint of a conversation about abusive relationships.

"Garrison…gave me a list of resources for where to go. He took me to a place, a home for women like me." Her eyes flittered away from Reyna to look outside the window. "It wasn't what I thought it would be. A dirty place with desperate and broken women who were too ugly to keep a man."

Reyna winced at the words that left her friend's mouth.

"The house is almost like mine," Marceline said. The one she'd given up in the divorce because she couldn't stand the memories it held for her. "It's big and airy and on the water. The women are nice. It's almost like they're at a retreat or something." A pained smile twitched across her face. "Garrison helped a lot of them. I can't thank you enough for talking to him for me. Without you, I'm not sure how all this would have turned out." Marceline took another deep breath.

"Anyway, I didn't come here to talk about me." She made a dismissive gesture. "Garrison is nothing like Ian." Reyna winced at the comparison between the two men. "He's so much better than that two-faced ass your ex turned into. Even though he never shares anything private with me, I can tell he wants things to work out between the two of you. You're the one who is pushing him away and—"

Reyna couldn't keep her mouth shut any longer. "You're wrong."

Marceline looked at her. "I've known you a long time, Reyna. Before Ian, you would've given a man like Garrison a chance. But the crap that happened when you were married changed you."

"If it hadn't been for Ian, I wouldn't have even *met* Garrison."

"You don't know that for sure. Not that it matters. Yes, he was the lawyer in your divorce, so what? Don't judge him from that first impression. If people met you at the tattoo studio and judged you based on that, it wouldn't be fair, either."

She winced at the mention of her job. "There's nothing wrong with what I do."

Marceline made a sound of frustration. "I wish you'd stop missing the point and hear what I'm telling you."

But Reyna's deflecting and dodging hadn't stopped her ears from working. "I hear you," she said softly.

After Marceline left, Louisa called. They tag-teamed her. In the most painful way possible, she reamed Reyna out for moping at the bar and ruining Marceline's fun.

"You need to get it together, friend," Louisa warned in that warm acid voice of hers. "I don't want to go hunting for *your* butt next time in a damn snow-storm."

With Louisa's words ringing in her ears, Reyna got ready for her job interview. Half her mind was focused on impressing the head of the graphic arts department. But the other was busy figuring out just exactly what she needed to do to fix things with Garrison. *If* they could be fixed.

Chapter 16

Reyna didn't allow herself to think too much about what she was doing. After her interview, she called to track Garrison down. Then she rushed home to shower and change, then rushed out again, this time taking an expensive cab ride into Manhattan.

She remembered where Garrison lived, and the doorman apparently remembered her, too. He gave her the same polite nod and smile he had the first and only time she visited the apartment, then held the door for her to pass into the opulent lobby.

In the elevator, the mirrored doors reflected a woman Reyna hadn't seen in a long time. Wild and sexy hair, red lips, eyes heavy-lidded and determined. She stood with her legs braced apart under a white summer trench coat. The black five-inch heels were higher than she'd normally wear, but they elongated her legs and made her feel painfully sexy. Or was it the tremor in her knees that caused the sweet ache?

She blinked at her reflection, and the woman in the mirror blinked back. There was no hint on her face of the nervousness she felt. A small mercy. When the elevator chimed, she took a quiet breath and stepped through the doors toward Garrison's apartment.

Reyna only gave herself a moment's quick breath before she rang the doorbell and settled her hands on the belt of her trench coat. She untied the belt just as the door opened, and propped her hands on her hips. Then she gasped. A strange man stood in the doorway of Garrison's apartment.

He was disturbingly beautiful. A better-looking Shemar Moore, with a shaved head, a goatee around his smiling mouth and bright white teeth. His dark eyes danced with friendly and flirtatious humor. Definitely not Garrison.

"Oh, my God!" Her face burned with embarrassment as she quickly gathered the edges of the coat together. "I'm so sorry! I—"

The man in the doorway grinned. "I'm not." His eyes were kind and sweet, although he did help himself to a second look at her figure, now safely covered up by the coat.

"I must be at the wrong apartment. I thought—"

"You're exactly where you need to be." He laughed again and called out over his shoulder, "I told you to get the door yourself, Garrison."

Reyna heard Garrison's deep voice call out from inside the apartment. Her face burned with mortification. She backed away from the door. "I'll just come back another time."

"Oh, no. You stay right there." The man shouted something else into the apartment that Reyna didn't understand. Something about Garrison dipping his oars in the water. He turned back to her. "I'm Wolfe, by the way. I'm sure I'll be seeing you again." He stepped back from the doorway and into the apartment.

Reyna heard voices rippling with amusement. Then a woman appeared in the threshold to flick her eyes once over Reyna before she glanced back at Wolfe. Reyna had a brief impression of gorgeous— short hair, model-sharp cheekbones, red lips—before the woman stepped back into the apartment. Moments later, she and Wolfe reappeared in the hallway.

At second glance, the woman was even more beautiful. She had a long and graceful neck, full lips and large eyes that reminded Reyna of a cat. She wore a designer black blouse, black pencil skirt and royal-blue high heels that rivaled the ones Reyna was wearing in height. And she was sure they were expensive.

"I'm just going to leave." Reyna clutched the edges of the trench coat tighter and turned to walk away. Heavy footsteps sounded near the door.

"Reyna?" Garrison stood in the doorway. "What are you doing here?"

But his eyes dropped to the trench coat, her stockinged legs, the high heels. His whole body went rigid, eyes devouring Reyna. She couldn't have moved if she wanted to. She licked her lips, goaded into the nervous habit, and Garrison's eyes latched on to the movement.

Reyna shivered.

"You're right, as usual," the woman said to Wolfe somewhere behind her.

Reyna was aware of the two strangers, but most of her was focused on Garrison.

"Garrison, Nichelle and I are heading out," Wolfe said. "We'll call you about brunch tomorrow."

She heard their footsteps leading away toward the elevators, but didn't watch them go. She couldn't take her eyes off Garrison.

"Come in." Garrison's voice was low and rough, a welcome abrasion.

She walked ahead of him into the apartment, vaguely aware of him closing and locking the door behind them. He said her name again and stepped closer.

"I've missed you," he said.

He gripped the edges of her coat in his fists, slowly parted the cloth. The balmy breeze from his apartment brushed over her skin, and she trembled.

"I need you."

The side of his mouth twitched at her words, but other than that, he was completely absorbed in looking at her.

The lingerie she wore was a pale green lace, like frosting on her body. The cups of the demi bra held up her breasts like fruit to whomever she wanted to have them, and the high-cut bikini panties elongated her legs even more. The stockings were black silk, held up by the pale green garter belt. His eyes stroked her; they did not tease, did not hint at things they had done, but raged with what he wanted to do to her. Her belly tightened.

When she'd left the house dressed in lingerie under

her trench coat, she thought of it as a naughty surprise to tease him with, to convince him to go out with her again, then they would talk and she would apologize and then... She couldn't think beyond that conversation. Only that she wanted the conversation to happen, and she needed him in her life again.

But now, with the incendiary heat of his eyes devouring her near-naked flesh, she didn't feel like talking. He said her name again and tugged the coat from her shoulders. Instantly, she felt naked. Soaked in her sudden and irrevocable arousal. This was not what she had planned, but now, with him watching her like a hawk that had sighted its prey, it was exactly what she needed.

He pulled her to him roughly, and she gasped, sucking in air and his breath then his lips. She moaned into the silken glide of his tongue and fit herself closer to him, sank her fingers into the back of his neck. His hardness pressed into her hip, and she moved against it, hungrily seeking. He groaned her name.

They caught fire together. She felt it. And it was perfect.

Garrison pulled away. "Before we do this—" His voice broke off. "Before we do this, you need to know I want more than tonight with you."

He sounded so sure of what he wanted, his gaze tearing her apart and putting her back together. Reyna made a low noise at the back of her throat, a whine of surrender and of yes, and of oh, God, why had she waited so long?

"Yes!" Reyna reached for him, her lips parted, hands sliding around his shoulders. "Yes. Please. That's what I want, too."

A quick confession tumbled from her, how much she wanted him but had fought against it out of fear. He stopped the rush of words with a finger against her lips. Reyna took the hint, but bit his finger, sucked it into her mouth and swirled her tongue around the thick hardness. Garrison's pupils widened, and his breath caught.

With a rough noise, he tugged the trench coat from her shoulders, threw it somewhere behind him. He swept her into his arms, and she shrieked softly with the surprise of it, her world spinning.

His bedroom was filled with sunlight and reminded her, strangely, of Halcyon. The big bed, dark furniture, the way he put her among the sheets like something precious. He shook his head like a man trying to clear a mental fog.

"I like your outfit." Garrison's voice was rough. He stood before her, leisurely tugging off his clothes as if he had all the time in the world. "But I'm afraid I'm going to take it off you now."

She mewled in anticipation.

Then he was naked, and a knee was pressing into the bed while she fought to take in all of him at once. The sculpted shoulders, hairless chest, solid abs and slight fuzz of a happy trail leading down to… She licked her lips.

And he touched her, very deliberately undoing the feminine magic of her lingerie, slipping off her stilettos, undoing the snap of her garter belts, rolling off her stockings. His fingers skated over her flesh, electric and warm. He was as deliberate about that as he was with everything else, and she whimpered with

arousal, the sweet heat building between her thighs
with every brush of his hands.

She didn't know when she was naked, only that
Garrison had unrestricted access to her body. He
touched her everywhere, deep and back-arching
strokes that made her moan his name.

She reached for him, adored his beautiful body
with her hands. The coiled muscles under silken skin,
the firmness of him, his mouth. He nipped her fingers with strong white teeth, and she gasped when
the sensation went straight to her core.

He smiled, a hard tilt of his mouth. "Payback."

A touch at the back of her knees made her legs fall
open for him. His breath brushed her ear in a filthy
whisper, then he slid deeply inside. She gasped at the
fullness of him.

Finally...

Her fingers dug into his hips to spur him on. But
Garrison did not rush. He stroked her languidly,
building a deliberate and pulse-pounding rhythm
that left her gasping. She held on tight as he loved
her, locked her ankles behind his back. The pleasure
rose in her as if it would never end.

"I love you!" She dug her nails into his back and
moved against the sheets. "I love you..."

He stuttered, and his hips froze their magical
dance between her thighs. He lifted his head to meet
her eyes.

"Reyna...?"

She whined and clutched at his hips, begging him
to move. "Please." She squirmed beneath him, pinned
to the bed where they were intimately joined. She
licked her lips at the expression on his face, hope-

ful and awed, a nakedness that had never been there before. Reyna said the words again and again and again. He closed his eyes and shuddered then drew back his hips, nearly abandoning the wet heat of her. She cried out again. He sank back into her, filling her with sweetness and more heat.

"Yes," she whispered. "Yes."

He bit her throat at the end of it and whispered something into her skin, something that her mind was too frayed to grasp while she lost her breath and all awareness of everything else to the sensations coursing through her body at the speed of light.

She must have slept, because the next thing she knew she was waking at Garrison's side, and all the lights outside the windows were muted. New York winked at her, a nighttime seductress. Garrison, sensing she was awake, shifted next to her, not seeming sleepy at all. His gaze swept over her face then her mouth. A shudder ran through him. But he only kissed her lips once before tugging her with intent from the bed and into the living room. More stars. More New York lights. Pinpricks of beauty piercing the darkness. Reyna sighed, feeling that all those lights, every single one outside the window, represented a piece of her happiness.

With a flick of his hand, Garrison turned on the lamps in the living room. He had draped a robe around her shoulders, silken and blue, and pulled on the pair of jeans he'd discarded earlier. On the sofa, he drew her to him, touching his forehead to hers. His warm breath teased her mouth.

"I want you again," he said. "I couldn't focus with you in my bed like that."

She bit her lip, pleased. "So the lingerie and trench coat…" She leaned into his steady strength and sighed when his arms wound around her from behind. "They were a success?"

His soft laugh floated above her head. Reyna twisted around to look into his face and see with her own eyes the laughter that transformed it. His eyes were warm and heavy-lidded, his mouth curved in a satisfied smile. Her heart knocked at the sight.

"Very much so," he said. "But I love you in anything. Naked. In a cabin. In New York. As long as you're with me."

At first, the words floated through her head as a pleasant and very positive response to her question. Then the one word knocked her in the belly like a hammer. *Love.*

She pulled away and sat up straight on the couch. "You love me?"

Reyna half expected him to make a denial about slips of the tongue or try to distract her with his hands. But he surprised her by allowing her to pull away. He sat beneath her shocked gaze, his face beautifully naked to her. "Yes, I do."

Reyna trembled at the certainty of his words. She propped her chin on her raised knees to watch him. He was so beautiful to look at, and she had been starved for him for so many months. He leaned back into the couch, circling her ankle with his fingers as if he needed that connection.

"I was actually on my way to see you." A wry smile touched his lips. "But, as usual, you surprised me." The pad of his thumb traced a line from her ankle down to her foot then back again.

The delicate movement stirred a flutter in Reyna's belly. He was so tender with her. With a start, she realized that he always had been. Their eyes met, and an expression moved over Garrison's face, a waiting. A thought. Then he apparently made a decision. He slid a hand into his jeans pocket. It emerged with a small silver box.

Reyna stilled.

"Before I saw you again at Halcyon, I never thought very much about partnership," Garrison said. "But once you and I started talking and you dug into the hidden parts of me, I saw things differently." He flipped open the box with his thumb.

The breath shivered in Reyna's throat. Her fingers, locked fiercely on her own arms, twitched. Inside the box lay a platinum necklace weighed down with a small Adinkra symbol. A grounded heart. Odo Nnyew Fie Kwan. The symbol that meant "love never loses its way home."

She swallowed the sudden lump in her throat. He remembered.

"I bought this for you at Halcyon." Garrison paused and lifted his gaze to Reyna. The lamps in the room highlighted his face, offering up every line, every angle to her. Nothing hidden. He licked his lips, an uncharacteristic gesture. "At the time, I wasn't sure what I meant when I bought this. I just had to let you know that the love your parents share can be yours, too." He touched her cheek with a hand that, incredibly, trembled. "But now...I know I want you to share it with me."

The feelings she had for him rolled over her like a tidal wave, undeniable. And she thought she'd have to convince him to give her another chance, but all the while… She picked up the necklace.

"All this time?" Her voice shook.

"Yes." The truth of his love poured from his eyes. Reyna allowed herself to look past his habitual reserve and see the fires in him that burned hotter than any she'd ever known.

He kissed the corners of her mouth, enveloping her with the scent of him, and of the two of them together. "All this time I've loved you, and you've only fought me, trying to get away to your lonely island."

"No. Never. I was just afraid of…of being hurt again." She wouldn't have been able to stand it if the thing she thought she had, unconditional and lasting love, turned out to be smoke and ashes. She did love him. Had loved him from the first. But she hadn't wanted to.

"There are few guarantees in life," he said.

"I know."

"But there *are* promises." He took her hand and placed it tenderly against his chest. "And there is this." His heart thundered beneath her hand. She closed her eyes and could swear she felt the rhythm of it in her own body. "I love you, Reyna Allen. I promise to be the best possible man I can be for you. Is that all right?"

"Yes," she said, breathless, tears falling. He kissed her wet cheeks and smiled when even more tears came. She laughed, throwing her arms around him. "It's more than all right with me."

Epilogue

Reyna slipped on her suit jacket and headed down the hall toward the elevator. She'd barely taken half a dozen steps, her high heels sinking into the thin carpet, before her cell phone rang. She smiled at the name and photo that popped up on the screen.

"Hi, love."

"Reyna."

Her hand reflexively tightened around the leather handle of her briefcase. Even after a year together, the way Garrison said her name still made her melt.

"I hope you left the office already," he said. "We're waiting for you at the restaurant." He sounded wonderfully relaxed. In the background, she could hear the sound of traffic, a car honking, as if he'd stepped away from the table to call her. "I didn't stop being a workaholic just for you to pick up my bad habits."

"No, never that." She laughed, shaking her head in denial, although he obviously couldn't see her. "A few last-minute things came up that I had to take care of."

Getting the job—complete with an office—at a downtown ad agency not far from where Garrison worked was a dream come true. The job had come on her own merit, and they worked her hard enough that she no longer thought of the position as a gift. Still, it was one of the most rewarding things she'd ever done.

"That's how it starts," Garrison teased. "And I would know."

"Yes," she murmured, picturing the curve of his smiling mouth. "You would."

Not long after they had made things official between them, Garrison started working less, wrapping up his workdays by six or seven in the evening, taking time to himself and actually relaxing for a change. He even made a spontaneous trip down to Florida to see Wolfe instead of being holed up in his admittedly beautiful study on a weekend when Reyna had to work.

One afternoon, while they lay on blankets on her living room floor, listening to music and basking in the sun, Garrison turned to her with mild surprise. "I forgot how good it feels to just do nothing," he said. Reyna laughed and pressed a kiss to his beautiful mouth. A week later, his secretary sent her a thank-you card.

"I'm leaving the office now." Reyna pressed the elevator button for the lobby. "I'll be there in—" she looked at her watch "—about thirty minutes if the train isn't acting up."

"Good. See you soon."

When she got to The Beautiful Feast about twenty-five minutes later, Vivian, the owner, greeted her with a warm smile at the door of the restaurant and waved her toward the private back room. The door was open, and she could hear the quiet conversations and laughter of her family and friends.

She stood in the doorway, watching them—Garrison talking gravely with her father while her mother showed something to Garrison's mother, Marian, on her smartphone. Louisa, Bridget and Marceline were all gathered around Wolfe, subtly vying for his attention. Her father saw her first.

"I'm impressed." He greeted her with a kiss and a teasing smile. "You're actually early. You must really think he's something special." He jerked his bearded chin toward Garrison.

Reyna turned her blushing face away to kiss Garrison. He palmed her hot cheek then gave her that small and intimate smile he reserved just for her. "The feeling is mutual, Mr. Allen." His warm breath brushed her throat, and she shivered in response, sliding her arms around his waist and inhaling his sensual, clean scent.

"Give the rest of us a chance," Wolfe said with a laugh.

When it was his turn, he enveloped Reyna in a warm hug. "Good to see you again, beautiful." He gave her that teasing once-over that made her shake her head before slipping neatly from his arms.

Marian Richards, whom Reyna had only spoken with a handful of times on the phone, stood up. "I finally get to meet the woman who captured my son's heart." Fine lines radiated from the corners of her expressive eyes when she smiled. She was as sensually attractive as her son, but her casual elegance—high heels, dark jeans and a white blazer—surprised Reyna. From what Garrison told her, she'd expected a bohemian in bright earrings and hemp harem pants.

"It's a pleasure to meet you, Ms. Richards." Reyna squeezed her extra tightly in thankfulness for the man she had raised her son to be.

"I already told you to call me Marian. The only Ms. Richards I know has a tombstone over her head in Tampa somewhere." Her smile took the sting from her words.

"Marian." Reyna squeezed her hands before slipping around the table to greet her mother.

"Baby, you look very Olivia Pope in that suit." Her mother named a character from a popular TV show she was obsessed with.

Reyna glanced down at her maroon skirt suit and black heels. "I thought she only wore white?"

Her mother shrugged. "That outfit is gorgeous and take-charge, and my baby is beautiful. Ergo, Olivia Pope."

Her father chuckled and gazed fondly at his wife. "She's just not used to seeing you in anything other than jeans. She's right, though, you look like a billion bucks."

Her father, a lover of word games of all sorts, was fond of hyperbole.

"Thanks, Daddy." Before her mother could say anything, she leaned over and kissed her powdered cheek. "You, too, Mama."

She quickly greeted her friends with hugs then started toward the chair Garrison was saving for her.

Bridget grabbed her hand en route. "Girl! You didn't tell me that Wolfe was so fine."

Reyna laughed. "I think he's taken."

"That's not what *he* said." Bridget raised a mischievous eyebrow, making plain her objective for the rest of the night. But Marceline, in her tight white dress, looked ready to give her some competition.

Garrison stood up and cleared his throat as Reyna sat next to him. There was an unfamiliar nervousness to him, an almost manic energy. "Thank you, everyone, for making the trek all the way here."

"Anything for you, honey." His mother smiled.

Garrison nodded and visibly pulled himself together. "I've already asked Reyna to marry me."

A collectively indrawn breath, Reyna's included, filled the room. She didn't think he would announce it quite like *this*. Her friends knew, but not their parents.

"She's accepted my proposal," Garrison continued, his voice falling into the commanding, I-*will*-get-my-way cadence he used at the office. He was nervous.

Reyna smiled and touched the engagement ring she wore on the chain with the Adinkra love charm he'd given her a year ago.

"Even though she hasn't said anything, I know she's still concerned about commitment." He glanced briefly at her, gifting her with that smile of his again. "So I invited you all here, the people we both love and trust, to pledge in front of you to always love this woman and always treat her heart as if it were my own. Fifty years, at least. That's what I asked her for, and that's what I'm telling you now."

Tears burned Reyna's eyes. She already knew their commitment was stronger than anything she'd had before—they spoke of a future together, of children, of the depth of their love for each other—but it humbled her that he wanted to make absolutely certain she trusted in the permanence of them.

"Wouldn't it be simpler to just marry her and make the same promise in front of God and everyone else?" Bridget pursed her lips.

"God is not going to drag him through Central Park and beat him with spiked Louboutins if he doesn't treat Reyna right," Louisa said with her martini glass raised to her lips. "But I will."

The parents stared at her.

"Exactly." Garrison winced. "But as you can imagine, I'm betting it won't come to that." He cleared his throat again. "And in any case, I will make that pledge to her in the church, but I want her to know my intentions before we get to that point." He touched Reyna's hand and met her eyes. "You're never getting rid of me," he said.

The tears she had been holding back spilled down her cheeks. "Why do you always make me cry?"

"I'm not sure this is a good start to forever, Garrison," his mother teased. But she was wiping away tears of her own.

Garrison cursed and jumped to his feet. His chair fell back and clattered to the ground. "I don't want you to cry, Reyna…" He enfolded her in a warm embrace. She burrowed into his body and clung, weeping.

"Let her get it out," she heard her mother say from her cocoon in Garrison's arms. "I haven't seen her cry like this since she was a child. Let her feel the sweet ache of loving you."

Reyna gasped on a sob. The feeling was almost too much. Her heart felt as if it was about to burst out of her chest.

"I feel like such an idiot for tearing up like this." She sniffed into his shirtfront and clung to the lapels of his blazer.

"But you're *my* idiot." He smiled against her cheek.

The door creaked open. "I thought this was supposed to be a celebration?" Vivian stood in the doorway with an open bottle of champagne and ten empty glasses. She was smiling.

"Congratulations, honey." Vivian put a warm hand on her back as she passed to distribute the champagne. "You found yourself a good one."

Reyna drew back to gaze into Garrison's smiling face. Her heart turned over in her chest and lay down completely for him. "I know."

* * * * *

Their passionate charade has become all too real!

Sin City
TEMPTATION

SHARON C. COOPER

Former police officer Trinity Layton will do anything to keep her personal security business afloat—even babysit professional poker player Gunner Brooks. But when the gorgeous playboy convinces her to pose as his girlfriend, she might be the one who needs protecting, as their chemistry sizzles. Now, as Gunner prepares for the championship of his career, he's playing for the highest stakes of all: Trinity's heart.

H HARLEQUIN®
™ www.Harlequin.com

Available March 2015!

REQUEST YOUR FREE BOOKS!

2 FREE NOVELS PLUS 2 FREE GIFTS!

KIMANI™
ROMANCE

Love's ultimate destination!

The first two
stories in the
Love in the Limelight
series, where four
unstoppable women
find fame, fortune
and ultimately…
true love.

LOVE IN THE LIMELIGHT

New York Times
bestselling author
BRENDA JACKSON
&
A.C. ARTHUR

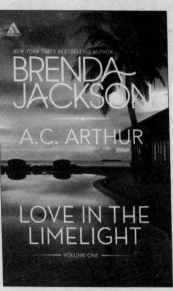

In *Star of His Heart,* Ethan Chambers is Hollywood's most eligible
bachelor. But when he meets his costar Rachel Wellesley, he suddenly
finds himself thinking twice about staying single.

In *Sing Your Pleasure,* Charlene Quinn has just landed a major
contract with L.A.'s hottest record label, working with none other than
Akil Hutton. Despite his gruff attitude, she finds herself powerfully
attracted to the driven music producer.

Available now wherever books are sold!

HARLEQUIN®
www.Harlequin.com

KPLIM11631014R

The last two
stories in the
Love in the Limelight
series, where four
unstoppable women
find fame, fortune and
ultimately…true love

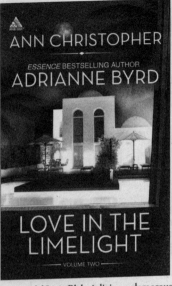

LOVE IN THE LIMELIGHT
— VOLUME TWO —

ANN CHRISTOPHER
&
ADRIANNE BYRD

In *Seduced on the Red Carpet*, supermodel Livia Blake is living a glamorous life…but when she meets sexy single father Hunter Chambers, she is tempted with desire and a life that she has never known.

In *Lovers Premiere*, Sofia Wellesley must cope as Limelight Entertainment prepares to merge with their biggest rival. Which means dealing with her worst enemy, Ram Jordan. So why is her traitorous heart clamoring for the man she hates most in the world?

Available now!

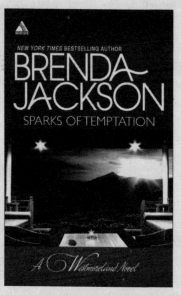

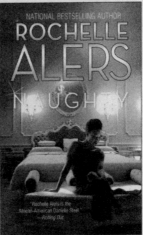